THE BETRAYAL OF JOEL

The Betrayal of Joel

Annie Lycett

This is a work of fiction. Names, characters, places, and incidents either are the product of the author's imagination or are used fictitiously. Any resemblance to actual persons, living or dead, events, or locales is entirely coincidental.

Copyright © 2023 by Annie Lycett

All rights reserved. No part of this book may be reproduced or used in any manner without written permission of the copyright owner except for the use of quotations in a book review.

First paperback edition 2023

978-1-80541-026-3 (paperback)
978-1-80541-027-0 (ebook)

This book is dedicated to the wonderful work of The Prince's Trust.

Darkness cannot drive out darkness; only light can do that.
Hate cannot drive out hate; only love can do that.

Martin Luther King, Jr.
(1929–1968)

CHAPTER ONE

Joel closed the kitchen drawer as quietly as he could, almost holding his breath, after retrieving the bread knife, which he carefully placed inside his rucksack after wrapping an old woolly jumper around its shiny, stainless steel blade. The next step was to negotiate his way past his mother who, after another night of consuming too much alcohol and smoking too many cigarettes, was sprawled, sylph-like upon the shabby sofa, where she would no doubt remain comatose for most of the day.

Silently, he rescued the remote control from her limp hand and turned down the volume on the television. Glancing momentarily at the screen, he observed the colourful pictures displaying a world completely alien to his own. Beautiful, bronzed people perched like preening peacocks in perfect palatial homes, wearing expensive designer clothes and driving the latest models of luxury cars through exotic locations, where golden sands stretched beside azure seas and which Joel could only imagine was "Paradise on Earth".

Such images were in stark contrast to those familiar in Joel's world, where all he knew were the grimy, grey walls covered in graffiti, the dark, cold, concrete stairwells, the broken lifts to the flat where he and his mother lived on the twelfth floor of the high-rise block, in an area known as one of the seedier parts of South London.

Once, the apartment block had been newly built and people praised the modern architects for their exciting futuristic vision. No one seemed to have considered that placing human beings in these domino-inspired blocks of concrete could kill the creativity and sensitivity of their souls.

As time passed and the council complained of lack of funds for the upkeep of the building, the tenants themselves, surrounded by the depressing state of their environment, began to suffer from depression. Relationships broke down and suicide rates increased as human beings reverted to their basic animalistic instincts.

Joel's father had originally envisaged the flat as their temporary home and with money saved in the bank, he had already taken Gemma and Joel to view large semi-detached houses in Wandsworth and Richmond. Gemma had even begun to imagine furnishing a home of their own. Joel's father had promised so much and sadly delivered nothing.

Joel's favourite pastime, since he was a young child, had been to stand on the small balcony of their flat and stare at the vastness of the city spread before him as far as his young eyes could see. He was fascinated by the endless jumble of roofs, skyscraper blocks, the space-aged Shard, all rising in different shapes and heights like a huge Lego city. Beyond, further into the distance and belonging to another, distant world, loomed the elegant shapes of classical church spires, the majestic and baroque St Paul's Cathedral, the Norman Tower of London; once fortress, palace, prison and the once regal remnants of a Roman wall, the proud protector of the city, now insignificant and barely noticed by citizens as its remnants appeared to gasp for air amidst the concrete jungle of monstrous, soulless shapes, threatening the ancient stonework as an alien army once had done.

Joel would imagine he could fly like Peter Pan over the night sky, illuminated by the lights flickering like fireflies against the backdrop of darkness, exploring the nooks and crannies of the vast cityscape. His Jamaican grandmother, whom he had adored, had saved her nurse's pension to take him, on his eighth birthday, to the West End to see *Peter Pan* and he had never forgotten the experience. The heavy plum-coloured velvet drapes hanging around the stage, the gilded ceilings where cherubs and angels, perched in the heavens, gazed down upon the audience, the plush maroon velour seats, the scent of his grandmother's eau de cologne, intermingled with the heavy incense of the theatrical space and combined with the powerful aroma of the actors' make-up was, as Proust might have remarked, a powerful and evocative memory, engraved forever in his soul.

His mother stirred; her brightly coloured kimono falling slightly open and revealing a glimpse of pale flesh. Joel winced; he must get out before she awoke, or she would start asking questions and want to know why he was late for school.

On the television programme, a glamorous actress, draped in silks and gold bangles, was being interviewed on the deck of a yacht in the Mediterranean. Joel vowed, there and then, that one day he would buy his mother a beautiful dress and gold jewellery and take her on a yacht, where she could lie in the sun overlooking the turquoise ocean.

Clutching his rucksack close to his chest, he crept past his sleeping mother and silently walked towards the front door. He carefully lifted the latch, closing it behind him, encountering the ginger cat, which had decided to enter through the cat flap at the same moment as Joel exited, almost causing him to trip over the feline creature.

"Stupid cat," Joel muttered to himself but he didn't have the heart to kick the cat as his father frequently used to do.

Joel quickly dismissed thoughts of his father, the father who once had been his hero, teaching Joel how to kick a ball into goal or play a chord on the guitar. The guitar had been given to his father for Joel by a member of the band for whom Joel's father acted as "roadie". The biggest treat for Joel had been standing at the side of the stage when the band was performing. The stentorian sound which penetrated the air space was so awe-inspiring that Joel felt immersed in its powerful magic. He imagined the coiled cables as slithering snakes, entwined and wriggling within the wires, wrapping themselves around the stage; a living art installation. The stadium full of adoring fans focused upon the musicians and chanting as if worshipping a group of mysterious gods. Joel could never imagine such hedonistic excitement which heightened his senses. He vowed to himself that one day he would stand upon such a stage, singing his heart out whilst the world looked on in admiration.

Sadly, these excursions came to an abrupt end when his father lost his job, having succumbed to the drug culture which permeated the music scene. Overnight, his personality changed and his handsome, dark-skinned father, whose dreadlocks framed his fine features like an exotic curtain and of whom Joel had been so immensely proud, became a stranger and a dealer in drugs.

Joel's beautiful blonde-haired mother, herself a catwalk model, always appearing so elegant, began drinking and smoking heavily. It was her way of retaliating and attempting to cope with the disintegration of her marriage; a marriage of which her middle-class parents in suburban Surrey had never approved and had refused to acknowledge their only grandson.

When Joel's father was arrested and sent to prison, Joel's mother refused to visit or to take her son anywhere near such a dark, depressing environment. When her husband was due to be released, she had packed a suitcase, thrown all his clothes inside and left it at the prison gate. Inside the case, she had written a note telling him not to bother coming home. Joel never set eyes on his father again and, as an eleven-year-old, felt both confused and betrayed. He made a promise to himself that he would never touch alcohol or drugs.

As Joel stood within the narrow confines of the bleak lift, which stank of stale beer and urine, he felt imprisoned in a miserable man-made environment with no hope of escape. He missed his father, when he allowed himself to remember the happy times they had spent together, but he had also seen how much his mother had been hurt and tried to understand why she would never have him back. There were many occasions when he cried himself to sleep, physically aching with longing for his father's strong arms around him and sometimes he almost hated his mother for sending him away.

She would say that Joel was the only man in her life now and she knew he would take care of her, to which he would reply that of course he would, but nevertheless it was a responsibility he could have done without. He knew he had let his mother down. Despite her perpetual drinking and drug taking, he still loved her and he knew she loved him.

"I went through more pain than I could have imagined possible to bring you into the world," she would taunt him playfully, with a large glass of wine in one hand and a spliff in the other, "And don't you ever forget it."

Her glazed pale blue eyes would pierce his as she stumbled against the shabby sofa. Joel knew she hated herself for taking the money he brought home to feed her habit but she never asked any questions. She had no need to as she knew exactly how it was acquired and she felt ashamed of herself for allowing her son to be a part of such an evil endeavour.

When her husband had left, she had every intention of staying clean herself, if only for Joel's sake, but when the modelling jobs dried up and money was tight, coupled with the fact that, as much as she adored Joel, her social life was non-existent, she had weakened and the occasional glass of wine and odd spliff soon increased to a bottle or two of wine and something stronger than hash.

Joel crossed the estate, smiling at old Muriel, who always sat snuggled in an old shawl on a bench beside the rubbish bins, despite the rancid stench which made Joel want to vomit. However, he knew her reason for choosing that same spot every day. By sitting there, she was always the first to know whether anything useful had been deposited in the bins or occasional skip. It could be scraps of unfinished takeaways or discarded pieces of furniture. Muriel never missed a trick!

She had been attacked several times by prowling burglars or hooligans clutching cans of lager but nothing deterred this eighty-nine-year-old; she had lived through the Blitz, of which she would proudly boast to anyone who would listen, and nothing could scare her more than Hitler's bombs destroying her home and killing her mother and baby brothers. Heaven knows why the young hooligans couldn't appreciate what they had today and realise that men as young as they were had sacrificed their lives to make the world a safer place. This was a familiar refrain she would repeat to anyone prepared to listen. Although from what she saw of life today, the world was sadly no longer a very safe place. Destruction was prevalent all over the planet, where wars raged consistently, crucifying countries and too often their innocent inhabitants.

"You take care now," Muriel called as Joel passed by. Her beady, brown eyes followed him protectively until he was out of sight.

To Muriel, he looked such a fine featured and innocent young lad but she was only too aware of the dangers lying in wait for youngsters today. She had already seen two young boys from the estate lose their lives.

Joel quickened his pace. Already late for school, he had forged a note from his mother in case he was asked. However, the chances were that no one would notice if he missed the first lesson, wandering casually into class for the second. The teachers were so over-worked they usually turned a blind eye to absentee pupils.

The second class was history and not Joel's favourite subject. All they ever studied were the First and Second World Wars, which Joel found so grey and depressing. He wanted to learn about ancient civilisations, eccentric kings and powerful queens, great writers and artists. The words "Renaissance" and "Age of Enlightenment" fired his imagination. When he enquired about the possibility of studying periods other than the two world wars, the response was that he could watch that sort of thing in films and on television. He thought he detected an air of disdain in the history teacher's voice, as if the distant past was mere fairy tales and really of no consequence today.

Joel entered the classroom to the cacophony of chattering voices and took a seat, placing the books he took from his rucksack on the table in front of him. He was aware of Jordan Cooper sitting behind him and sensed his menacing black eyes burning into his back, a torturer holding a red hot poker against his flesh. He knew that at the end of the lesson Jordan would choose his moment to pass him a small parcel with instructions placed inside, which were to be memorised and destroyed. Joel also knew it was more than his life was worth to refuse to take it. He felt trapped as an animal of prey with no means of escape.

Joel had resolved from a very young age never to touch drugs; he had witnessed the devastating effect upon his parents' lives. However, he knew he could not refuse the addicts and dealers in his class who had him marked as their go-between. With his dark curly hair and innocent brown eyes, they knew he would be beyond suspicion. They assured him that as long as he kept his mouth shut and did as he was told, he would come to no harm. He was also promised the chance to earn regular money for his services.

Joel was only too aware of his mother's anxiety about unpaid bills and bailiffs pounding on their front door, causing even more of the remaining paint to peel and crack.

At first, when she had refused to have his father back, she had appeared to manage. Her parents, now both dead, had not left her anything in their will and she relied upon money earned from modelling jobs to provide for herself and Joel. However, as the alcohol and drugs took hold, her looks began to fade and the agencies stopped calling her for work.

When he first saw the look of relief on his mother's tired face as he handed over the first bundle of notes, Joel felt it was worthwhile. He knew a young Somalian boy in his class was doing exactly the same for his mother and brothers, who would go without food, heating and clothes were it not for the drug money he earned.

"Hold on." Jordan Cooper forcefully took hold of Joel's jacket as he stood up to leave the classroom. "Not so fast. Meet me in the toilets *now*," he hissed between his rotten teeth resembling a dangerous serpent who had captured his prey.

Joel nodded and with a glance at the teacher, Miss Winter, who seemed to be looking in his direction, he picked up his books and left the room, heading along the corridor.

As he entered the toilets, which always smelt disgusting and where the cleaners fought a constant battle in trying to clean the lewd graffiti from the walls, he headed for a cubicle at the far end where Jordan was waiting for him.

"Here." Jordan shoved an envelope into Joel's hands. "Deliver to Bigsy."

"How will I know him?" Joel asked, trying to avoid the hard look in Jordan's eyes.

"You'll know him, all right. He'll be waiting for you round the back of the South Bank... Big bloke covered in tattoos, even his prick. Not that you want him to be showing you that." He let out a crude chuckle.

"That's miles away from Elephant and Castle."

"No, it ain't... what does his lordship expect, a taxi?"

The sound of footsteps alerted them to a master entering the toilets.

"Quick. Scarper as soon as he's had a piss," Jordan commanded.

Both boys remained silently in the cubicle with Joel aware of Jordan's foul-smelling breath next to his face. As soon as the master had finished, they returned to the corridor with Joel clutching his rucksack to his body, knowing he must not lose the parcel inside it.

When the lunch bell rang, he left the school grounds and walked to the tube station, studying the map for which tube train went to Waterloo.

Walking along the South Bank, he admired the sight of the grand buildings bordering the River Thames on the opposite side. He imagined how much history their walls had witnessed since they were first built. There would have been elegant parties where guests, attired in velvets and silks, wafted up and down the grand ornate staircases and danced in the marble floored ballrooms, before dining upon exotic dishes by candlelight. A few generations later, these same rooms would host more serious gatherings where men, dressed in smart pin-striped suits and wearing old school ties, would hold financial meetings or discuss the progress of the world wars, well aware that both the buildings and they themselves were vulnerable to Hitler's bombs at any time.

Today, these architectural gems were mainly offices, inhabited by VIPs engaged in governing the country and not, in Joel's opinion, making a very good job of it. Otherwise, kids like him would not get involved in drug dealing.

Joel thought it unfair that people involved in manual labour, often dirty and dangerous work, and nurses and doctors and school teachers, educating the future generation, could only dream of the opulent and luxurious lifestyles of a privileged few who had, by birth or good fortune, accumulated an unfair proportion of the wealth. As Rousseau had stated in the book which Joel's English teacher had quoted during class the previous week, "Property and lavish lifestyles divided society, breeding envy and discontent," and went on to say that we should all care for each other, not just in our own country but for all our brothers and sisters everywhere. Joel had thought of Leila, a young Yazidi girl in his class, and how hard life had been for her and her family who had fled to England as asylum seekers.

Joel arrived at his destination and what a contrast this was: dingy, damp, dirty hovels where squatters had made temporary homes, no better than those similarly inhabited in the Victorian underworld. Graffiti-covered walls of corrugated iron, cardboard and old torn sheets and curtains added to the general state of dilapidation.

Later, in the early evening, men and women, attired in evening dress and dinner suits, would make their way into the various theatres and concert halls along the South Bank where they would order champagne for the interval and, as they sipped from their glass, would gaze at the magical lights across the river, twinkling as if in competition with the stars in the night sky. These concert and theatre goers were no doubt oblivious to the forgotten souls just a few minutes away, hungry, shivering, attempting to sleep upon hard, cold, concrete floors and drinking themselves into an early grave, trying to forget their fruitless existence of permanent unhappiness.

Joel stepped hesitantly beneath an arch where the stale stench of body odour, leftover food cartons and urine, mixed with drugs and alcohol, made him want to throw up.

He was wondering which direction he should take when he was suddenly confronted by a dark-skinned figure who towered like a giant above him. His beard was unkempt and grew, like Medusa's snaky hair, from his chin to his chest. He was dressed in cheap, black leather and there was a menacing air about his demeanour.

He watched Joel approach and beckoned him with a filthy, bent finger.

"Got something for me?" he growled, holding out his thick, ugly hand. His huge body exuded a vile smell of putrid flesh. Any inch of flesh showing was covered in tattoos, just as Jordan had described.

Joel stopped abruptly. He felt small and insignificant before this colossus of a man. Nervously, he put his hand in his rucksack and pulled out the brown envelope which Jordan had thrust into his hand earlier.

The man snatched the package.

"Cool," he snarled unsmiling and, turning on his heels, disappeared further inside the dark interior.

Joel watched him disappear and then started walking back the way he had come. If he was quick enough, he could make it in time for afternoon lessons.

CHAPTER TWO

Back in the classroom, Jordan turned and gave Joel a thumbs up. Joel wondered when he would get paid. After all, the man he had met had not given him any money. He supposed he and Jordan had some sort of agreement.

At the end of school, Joel lingered in the corridor.

"Okay, man?" Jordan swaggered into view.

Joel nodded.

"So, what are you waiting 'ere for? Was you expecting somefing?"

"My money," Joel almost whispered, afraid of Jordan's wrath.

"Oh yeah, sorry, almost forgot." Jordan smirked, taking a wad of notes out of his trouser pocket and pressing them into Joel's hand. "First instalment." He grinned, enjoying his moment of power. "But I'm warning you, don't go gettin' greedy or it'll end in tears."

He strode past Joel, deliberately brushing against him as he headed for the exit doors.

Joel heaved a sigh of relief as he deposited the notes in his rucksack; he would count them when he arrived home.

✦ ✦ ✦

His mother was preparing supper when he walked through the door. Joel was relieved she was up and cooking, instead of lying on the sofa in her usual lacklustre state.

"Hello, darling." She turned and smiled at him. "Good day at school?"

Joel briefly brushed his lips against her pale cheek and handed her the bundle of notes.

"Thanks, love," she said, walking over to an old bread bin and dropping the money inside. "I hope you're being careful, sweetheart." She turned back to face him. "I couldn't bear it if you got into trouble."

"It's okay, Mum. I can look after myself." He couldn't help but wonder why, when she refused to take her husband back after his drug dealing, she allowed her son to deal.

His mother smiled at him. "You're very precious to me, you know."

She stepped forwards about to hug him but he had already turned away and was taking off his school blazer and hanging it on a peg in the tiny hallway. His young mind was confused. He knew she loved him but he also knew she relied upon his money, so what choice did he have but to keep doing whatever Jordan Cooper ordered him to do. He knew he was too deeply involved now. If he refused Jordan, he would become another victim found with a blade in his chest.

He still did not understand why Jordan and his cohorts had chosen him to be their runner. He supposed it was because everyone called him baby face and adults thought he looked angelic and innocent; no one would suspect him of trafficking drugs. Being small for his age, people thought he was younger than his fourteen years.

He would never forget the first time Jordan and the gang leader, who was much older, had stopped him outside the school gates and insisted upon accompanying him home. On the way, they had said they had a proposition which would change his life and enable him to look after his mother. They explained he needed to pass a test first and told him to meet them at 7 o'clock that evening near Clapham Common.

Joel never left his mother alone in the evening, unless he had an after-school activity, which he rarely did as he was worried about her. Occasionally, she herself ventured out to "see friends" as she called them, leaving Joel to his own devices.

That particular evening, she was not going out and therefore he had to lie, saying he had an evening class at school.

Whether or not she believed him was hard to tell and he had left her working her way through a bottle of gin and chain smoking her way through a packet of cigarettes.

Joel arrived on the common just as the sun was slowly setting in a haze of pinks, purples, bright orange and blues beyond the treetops. The bright light darted amidst the dark, leafy branches of the trees, making magical patterns against the luminous backdrop.

Momentarily, he had stood in awe, staring at the blaze of coloured sky. He thought how like a painting it was, as if some master artist had swept his brush across the sky, having dipped it into every colour upon his palette. For a brief second, he experienced a feeling of happiness and a belief that the world could be a place of joy.

These optimistic thoughts were soon shattered, however, as he saw the menacing duo standing in wait beneath a giant oak.

The older man, whom he had seen occasionally at the school gates and whose dreadlocks hung halfway down his back, appeared to be clutching some sort of metal chain in one hand and smoking a spliff with the other. When he opened his mouth, a gold tooth glinted in the evening light. A deep scar was engraved from eye to ear on his left cheek. Joel would have cast him as the villain in a horror film. Beside him stood Jordan, looking pale and anxious as if awaiting his doom; his habitual nervous twitch more accentuated than ever.

The older man stepped forwards. Joel couldn't take his eyes off the gold teeth and then noticed a gold earring in his ear too. He'd have made a good pirate, he thought.

"Right, you must be Joel," he growled.

Joel nodded.

"Jordon tells me we can trust you."

Joel nodded again, about to say yes but the words wouldn't come out.

"See that pub?" He pointed to a public house across from the common and Joel noticed more gold on his fingers.

Joel nodded again nervously and this time managed a yes, which came out rather squeakily.

"We want you to go in there and nick as many wallets, handbags and purses as you can in the next half hour. Understood?"

If Joel hadn't been so scared, he would have laughed as this sounded like some TV quiz show. He knew he had no choice but to do as the man said. He did mutter something about being underage and probably looked even younger than he was but it didn't seem to bother them.

"Pull your hoody up and ask for an orange juice. Tell them you're waiting for your mum," he barked. "Now beat it… we're timing you."

Joel walked reluctantly towards the pub entrance. There were quite a few drinkers seated at tables outside smoking. He entered the bar area where men and women were seated in a far corner, laughing and engaged in a pub quiz.

He decided at first just to sit near this group, who were rather loud, and watch them for a while. If they were distracted in answering questions, he could seize the chance to relieve them of their wallets or snatch the women's handbags, although he wasn't sure how exactly he would do this as he had never stolen anything in his life. Not even a chocolate bar from the local corner store, despite all the other kids on the estate frequently filling their pockets.

In the opposite corner, there was a television showing a football match. If anyone challenged him, he would say he had come in to watch the game. Fortunately, at the moment, the bar staff seemed fully occupied pouring drinks and serving food to the clientele.

Joel decided to sit near the huge television, slightly hidden by a pillar but with a view of the screen. He looked around; his palms were sweating. Female companions of the football fans had tucked their bags beside their feet, half-hidden under the tables, where they sat with their drinks as they chatted animatedly to each other. Joel hadn't a clue how he could take a bag without it being noticed and then he'd be in real trouble. He did not want to end up in prison like his dad.

He contemplated lifting wallets from the back pockets of the men's trousers whilst they were engrossed in the match, but supposing they felt him doing it and turned to confront him!

He was about to give up, resigned to his fate when Jordan and his accomplice discovered he was a failure. Perhaps they would decide he wasn't suitable for their purpose and would leave him alone.

Pulling his hoody over his head and putting his hands in his pockets, he stood up, ready to make his getaway.

Just as he was about to pass through the door, his eyes fell upon an open shoulder bag hung on the back of a chair.

The owner, an attractive fair-haired young woman wearing a chic leather jacket, was in animated conversation with a handsome young man, whom Joel assumed was her boyfriend from the way they each seemed transfixed, gazing into each other's eyes. This was his last chance.

Quietly, he took a step back and casually lowered his right arm towards the open bag. Luckily for him, the purse was perched just inside as if inviting a thief to take it.

Within two seconds, Joel had the designer purse within his grasp and in another second, he had fled from the pub and was pounding across the common, his heart beating faster than he had ever known before.

Jordan and his companion were sitting on the grass puffing at spliffs at the spot where Joel had left them.

"How did it go, man?" the gang leader had asked, a tone of menace in his voice.

"Sorry, guys, I only got one purse." He handed the trophy over to the leader's outstretched hand.

"At least you're not empty handed," Jordan said, sounding almost as if he was on Joel's side as the older man grunted. "Gucci too, man."

Growler was already unclipping the large clasp and emptying the contents and Joel sighed with relief as a huge grin crossed the man's face, stretching the scarred skin, which added to his somewhat terrifying appearance.

"Jammy bugger... you must 'ave picked the best wallet in the pub, man. Look at all these gold cards, not to mention wads of notes. Was she a duchess or somink?"

"I dunno," Joel retorted. He had felt sick in the pit of his stomach, not to mention ashamed. "She was very pretty."

The pair started to laugh; the older man's shoulders shaking and the tattooed tiger, its teeth on his left arm, gave an illusion of biting into his sallow skin.

"Very pretty, eh? Cute, man." He was still counting the notes. "Well, she weren't short of a penny or two. Must have been on her way to the bank or up to something well dodgy. There's a thousand nicker 'ere."

Joel began to wonder whether he had stolen her month's rent or perhaps money she had been saving for something special. He wished he could turn round and take it back to her but, of course, that was impossible.

"Growler", as he had just heard Jordan call the man, was throwing out car keys and house keys.

"If we could get an address amongst this stuff, we could tell the lads to do a quick break in," he said, pleased with himself.

"Have to be quick though," Jordan warned, "She's probably reporting it to the police at this very moment."

"Can we go now?" Joel had asked. He was shivering both from fear and cold and wanted to get away from this place as soon as possible. The sun had gone down long ago and there was a cool breeze.

"Yeah, scarper," Growler shouted.

Joel had assumed they would be accompanying him back but they obviously had other plans. He began to walk slowly away from them, hoping he could remember the way they had come. It had seemed a long way from his estate and he knew his mother would be starting to worry by now and his mobile battery was flat.

He had noticed the contrast between this neighbourhood and where he had come from. Some roads consisted of large period houses with expensive cars parked in the drives and trees and shrubs surrounding the exteriors. Occasionally, he passed a smart restaurant where smells of delicious culinary delights wafted into the night air. Looking through the windows, he saw smartly dressed diners seated at candlelit tables, enjoying their meals. One day, he thought, he would like to bring his mother to eat in a place like one of these, just once. He knew, of course, that when she was younger and with his father, they probably ate at such establishments but that had been a long time ago.

Lowering his eyes to the pavement, Joel remembered the pretty girl whose bag he had stolen. She had seemed so happy, throwing her head back so that her silky blonde hair brushed the back of her shoulders and she would flick a few strands with her fingers in a flirting gesture as she chatted and laughed with her companion.

He tried to picture her now and the scene in the pub, no doubt of panic and disbelief, probably in shock, realising all her money, credit cards and house keys had gone. He imagined her tearful face and as he did so, tears trickled down his cheeks.

When Joel eventually arrived back at the estate, the lift was out of order. Upon entering the grim, gun metal stairwell, he began the long climb to the twelfth floor, holding his nose for as long as he could in an attempt not to smell the stench of the rubbish, human waste and general detritus scattered on the concrete steps.

When he walked into the flat, he did not know whether to be disappointed or relieved that his mother was not awake worrying about where he was but instead she lay, dead to the world, on the sofa, an empty bottle of gin lying on the floor beside her and a movie on the TV playing to itself.

Wearily, Joel fetched the duvet from her bedroom and gently placed it over her sleeping body. He then returned to his own bed, praying for the oblivion which he hoped sleep would bring. Gently, he removed the knife from under his sweatshirt and, placing it under his pillow, heaved a sigh of relief that he had not had cause to use it.

Unsurprisingly, Joel could not sleep. When he did appear to drift into the world of dreams, he was consumed by nightmare scenarios where he was standing in the centre of a room with drunken revellers surrounding him and pouring cans of beer over his head, so that he could not avoid the putrid taste in his mouth. Looking down to the floor, he noticed his feet were submerged in a pool of stale beer and urine. Somehow, he managed to extricate himself from the scene, only to be chased down the street by armed police chanting, "Thief, thief!"

When eventually they caught up with him, they found the knife he was hiding and, taking it from him, they began to thrust it into his flesh, threatening to cut him up into little pieces, which the drug dealer, standing nearby, was waiting to eat.

"Oh, gross!" Joel awoke with a start thinking he was going to vomit.

His mother was calling from the kitchen and the smell of bacon wafted into his bedroom. Normally, he would have looked forward to one of the rare breakfasts his mother cooked but this morning he knew it would be an ordeal to get through it.

Dragging himself out of bed, he checked the knife was still under his pillow. He transferred it to under the bed, after wrapping it in the jumper, just in case his mother decided to make his bed whilst he ate his breakfast. This was highly unlikely but better to play it safe.

"Smells good, Mum," Joel lied as he sat at the Formica kitchen table, trying not to throw up with each mouthful of bacon.

His mother joined him at the table. "What time did you come in? I must have drifted off to sleep."

For someone who had consumed a bottle of gin, she seemed surprisingly lucid.

"Yeah, you were asleep when I came in. Sorry, it took longer than I thought."

She poured herself a cup of tea. One habit she had retained from her middle-class parents was to brew tea in a pot and not resort to tea bags.

"Joel," she said.

"Yes, Mum?"

"You're not in any kind of trouble, are you? I mean, I know the money you make on the side manages to keep us afloat but I'd hate to think you were putting yourself in any danger." She stirred a large spoonful of sugar into her tea.

"Mum, I can look after myself, okay?"

Gemma sipped her tea, her trembling hands clutched around the mug. "I know I let you down, Joel. I'm sorry. I should go to the job centre again but I'll probably end up earning less than I get in benefits."

Joel finished his bacon which he'd placed between two thick slices of bread. He realised how hungry he had been despite the sick feeling which still lingered in his stomach.

"I don't suppose you've got any spare cash, have you, love?" she asked, embarrassed.

"Mum, I gave you all that money yesterday. You can't have spent it already!" Joel stared across at her in disbelief.

Gemma looked sheepish and, taking a packet of cigarettes from her dressing gown pocket, lit one, blowing a circle of smoke into the air causing Joel to feel nauseous again.

"Not all of it but the rent's due and the electric."

"You can't afford to buy cigarettes," Joel said crossly, "And they'll kill you. It's mad! And the alcohol..." His voice drifted off.

She stretched her arm across the table and laid her hand upon his, then almost pleadingly said, "Please, baby, what other pleasures do I have stuck here all day? Don't begrudge me a drink or a smoke."

Joel was about to launch into a diatribe about how selfish she was to expect him to work for drug dealers to pay for her addictions but he knew it would only end in a scene where she would burst into tears, apologising for being such a failure and begging his forgiveness, saying he'd be better off without her.

He drew his hand away, stood up and took his plate to the sink. "I have to go to school."

He turned and went into the bathroom. Turning on the tap, he wished he could wash away the bad deeds which he had committed, just as Lady Macbeth had attempted to do in the play they were studying at school but then she didn't have much success either!

Jordan was waiting for him in the school cloakroom.

"Joel," he called, stopping him with an outstretched arm as Joel attempted to walk past. "Jus' wanted to say well done, man, for the other night. Growler is well impressed and wants to upgrade you."

"What?" Joel retorted, not sure he understood what being upgraded meant in the world of drug dealing.

"Upgrade, you know, bigger jobs, more money..."

"Like what?" Joel sounded anxious.

"Like bigger deals, stronger stuff... no need for you to worry your little 'ead about it. You'll get instructions."

"And what if I don't want to?" Joel was feeling nauseous.

Jordan shrugged. "You don't mess with Growler. What he says, you do. Don't look so worried. Think about all the dosh and what you can buy, man... the best trainers, Gucci loafers..."

"I'm not interested in clothes," Joel said.

"Yeah, well, can't say I hadn't noticed." Jordan looked down his nose like a haughty horse. "You have to look the part though."

"The only reason I do this is to help my mum pay the bills and buy food."

"Where's your old man then?"

"Not around."

"Scarpered, did 'e?" Jordan studied the look on Joel's face. He was a perceptive boy when it came to summing up other people. "In trouble, is he?" There was almost a note of sympathy in his voice.

"He was," Joel said quietly.

"In prison?"

"Yes."

"What for?"

"What do you think?"

"Dealing?" Jordan asked, half-joking.

Joel nodded.

"Oh, well, chip off the old block then." He could see Joel was upset. "Sorry," he said quickly, "That's tough, man."

"And yours?"

For the first time, Joel wondered what Jordan's background was. He wasn't bad looking. In fact, many of the girls in class fancied him. Some of them said he bore a resemblance to Tom Hardy, the actor whom they all fancied. He walked with a swagger to give the impression of confidence, although Joel suspected that in reality it was to cover up his insecurity. He was intelligent too, quietly gaining good grades but not wanting anyone to notice.

"Stabbed, weren't 'e," he stated in a matter-of-fact manner.

"Badly?" Joel asked innocently.

"If you call 'to death' pretty bad, yeah." Jordan's lower lip began to quiver and he cast his eyes down to the ground, wanting to avoid Joel's gaze.

Joel hesitated before asking, "Do you miss him?"

"Nah, I can't remember a lot about him now. He used to take me sister and me out when we were little kids but then he sort of lost interest..." His voice trailed off and Joel said no more. He suspected Jordan had suffered more pain in his short life than he cared to admit.

Fellow pupils were brushing past the pair on their way to classes after the bell had gone.

A male teacher approached. "Haven't you two got lessons to go to?" he barked.

"Yes, sir. Sorry, sir." It was Joel who spoke as he turned to go.

Defiantly, Jordan took his time. Joel felt like a lamb being led to the slaughter. From now on, he was trapped in an inevitable life of crime.

When Joel was engrossed in a subject, he managed to forget about his "other life" as he thought of it. This was especially true in English when they studied and performed plays, which they were doing at the moment, with Shakespeare's *Macbeth*. Joel had been cast as Banquo, which he was thoroughly enjoying and the fact that he reappeared as a ghost was even more exciting.

He always looked forward to art classes too, although he did not profess to be a budding Picasso, he enjoyed the escapism which drawing and painting provided. When Miss Wells, the wonderfully eccentric art teacher, wafted into the art studio, the class waited in anticipation. Today, Eleanor was attired as a bohemian hippie from the sixties, complete with long, dangling earrings, which sparkled each time she tilted her head, and necklaces of rainbow-coloured stones draped around her neck. Her arms were arrayed with silver and copper bracelets and beaded bangles which jangled whenever she lifted a hand, gesturing for silence. She had acquired much of her decorative jewellery from her trips to India, a country she adored and which never failed to fascinate her. In addition to visiting the famous landmarks, palaces and the Taj Mahal, Eleanor would spend time at yoga retreats in remote parts of the countryside where she discovered a deep sense of spirituality, which never failed to fill her with renewed hope and optimism for the future.

She then announced she would be taking the class to the National Gallery. Joel was genuinely excited. He thought he had heard of the National Gallery but nonetheless was relieved when another boy asked whether this meant getting a train out of London. Miss Wells explained that the art gallery was not very far away but in the heart of London, overlooking a square named after a battle between the British Navy against France and Spain during the Napoleonic Wars. The battle took place in October 1805 off the coast of Cape Trafalgar; hence the name Trafalgar Square.

None of the class had ever seen genuine paintings before. At home, Joel's mother had a few framed prints on the walls, including one of a group of people dressed in colourful old-fashioned costumes seated on a boat at dining table. The table displayed elegant wine glasses and half empty bottles of wine and champagne and the remains of what appeared to be an excellent lunch. One young woman, wearing a straw hat decorated with a ribbon and flowers, was cuddling a black fluffy dog, who was seated upon the table. Gemma had said the original was by a French painter named Renoir. Another print depicted naked ladies bathing in a marble floored hall, whilst other characters wore white, floating, Roman dresses. The original painting was by someone with a double-barrelled name, which he couldn't remember. Joel had been fascinated by the naked bodies of the women, however. The thought of seeing the actual paintings which the artists had created with their own brushes was something else.

He was relieved he could pay the cost of the outing and had no need to ask his mother for money.

CHAPTER THREE

On the day of the outing, Joel was up earlier than usual, despite having been out late the night before delivering more packages for Jordan and Growler.

It had not been the usual sort of place which Joel had been sent to. The large double fronted house was in a smart road on the opposite side of the common from the pub where Joel had stolen the Gucci wallet.

He still felt guilty about the young woman and often thought about her before he went to sleep at night, wondering whether she was still upset and how much the money had meant to her. He hoped he did not see her when he was passing the pub!

He walked into the tree lined driveway where more expensive cars than he had ever seen in his life were parked side by side; a shiny black Porsche nuzzled against a bright red Ferrari. How Joel would have loved to sit in the driver's seat and clutch the steering wheel in a moment of childhood fantasy.

When he knocked on the oak front door, he had a good view through the large bay window to his right and could see a high-ceilinged room where women in expensive-looking dresses and men in smart suits stood chatting and laughing with each other. They all appeared to be holding glasses in their hands, which several hovering waiters kept topped up with Premier Cru champagne.

As the door was opened by a house maid dressed in black dress and white apron, the sound of loud laughter and animated conversation echoed in the massive mosaic tiled hallway.

"Yes?" The petite woman looked Joel up and down as if instinctively knowing he had not come to the party, even as someone's son.

Upon Jordan's advice, he had worn a smart jacket over his black school trousers. It was too tight and the sleeves too short and it had remained in the cupboard from the day his mother had bought it for him in the sales, but it was smarter than his bomber jacket.

Joel awkwardly shuffled his feet. "I have a package to deliver," he said, wondering whether to take it out of his rucksack and hand it to her.

He was afraid she would ask who it was for as he did not have a name, but she seemed to be expecting it.

"I'll take it," she said, almost snatching the package from his hand and promptly closing the door in his face.

Joel had walked as fast as he could and was relieved to get back to familiar territory.

Today, he decided he was going to banish all bad thoughts and concentrate upon the wonderful paintings he was going to see.

He made himself a bowl of cornflakes, as his mother was still asleep, and crept out of the flat.

The class met in the art studio and Miss Wells counted all twenty-five pupils were present.

"Now remember," she said, "To be considerate and make way for other pavement users at all times. Are we ready?"

"Miss, I need a piss." It was Jamal who spoke. "Sorry, miss."

Jordan heaved a sigh and threw him a look of frustration.

"All right. Well, be as quick as you can," Eleanor said. "Now, does anyone else need the toilet before we leave?"

Two giggling girls, whom the English teacher had christened Rosencrantz and Guildenstern after the foppish pair who seemed indistinguishable in Shakespeare's *Hamlet*, raised their hands. They had put lipstick and mascara on to celebrate a day away from school.

When everyone was present, Eleanor led them out of the school and across the common to the underground station resembling the Pied Piper leading her flock.

Her appearance was as exotic as ever: a floating, floral kaftan depicting birds of paradise covered her black leggings and fell just above her red, suede booties. Her long, dark hair, which normally showed signs of grey, was tucked into a pale blue, silk turban, complemented by turquoise earrings dangling from her ears. Joel thought she looked like a living work of art and, judging by the glances she was getting on the way to the tube, other people thought this too.

They were a noisy band of boys and girls, chattering with excitement to be away from the school grounds and alighting in the bright sunshine at Charing Cross before walking across the impressive Trafalgar Square. Tourists gathered to take selfies and admire the statue of Nelson who stood statesman-like, looking down upon the fountains from his massive stone column with slightly scary sculptured lions guarding him below.

It was exciting to be transported to the heart of London with its famous sites. Through an impressive archway to one side of the square, they could see the Mall, which led to Buckingham Palace where the queen lived.

Joel was fascinated by the crowds, consisting of many nationalities and speaking in many different languages, a twenty-first century "Tower of Babel". These tourists watched enthralled as street artists created chalk pictures upon the pavement slabs and mime artists stood still as statues in various poses, whilst magicians performed their tricks in the centre of a magic circle, drawing gasps from the admiring audience. There were musicians playing intriguing instruments of various size and sound, all adding to the colourful spectacle and lively atmosphere. Joel felt it was as if he were looking at a kaleidoscope of all humanity.

For Joel and his classmates, this was another world, far away from the drab estates and graffiti-covered walls, which most of them were used to.

The imposing building, which was the National Gallery, stood proud and impressive, looking over the square where the fountains flung transparent streams of water resembling gossamer wings of dancing fairies, enhancing the magical atmosphere of the surroundings.

Joel was enthralled as they all leapt up the steps to the main entrance; Miss Wells and her assistant attempting to keep up with them.

Some of the group were just enjoying being away from school for the day. Looking at paintings did not appeal to them, although one or two showed a real talent for painting.

Inside, they gazed in wonder at the high ceilings as they explored the grand interior.

"Are these real pictures, miss?" a young female student asked, as she moved closer to the rope which prevented anyone getting too close. As if spellbound, she gazed up at a large oil painting depicting figures taking afternoon tea in a glorious colourful garden.

"Indeed they are." Miss Wells smiled. "These people had amazing talent for transposing their subjects from reality onto canvas. Which doesn't mean to say you aren't capable of having that talent as well."

Leila was a striking girl. She had come to the UK with her aunt and mother and baby brother and sister. The family was Yazidi, originally from Yemen and then the Sinjar area of northern Iraq from where they had been forced to flee when the Islamic state invaded their territory and thousands of Yazidi men were killed and boys as young as nine taken to be trained as child soldiers. Their people had a history of being persecuted and suffering from horrendous attacks from ISIL, who regarded them as devil worshippers due to their ancient religion. They had suffered constant persecution; children and adults had been slaughtered. Their pleas for mercy ignored.

In 2007, hundreds of Yazidi had been killed in car bomb attacks after the American invasion. Women and children were raped, enslaved; young children torn from their mothers' arms.

There was no water or food for the babies who were dying in their hundreds. It was in Iraq that Leila's father, a respected surgeon, refused to leave the operating theatre and continued to save lives until a bomb destroyed the hospital. He died along with his patients, whose lives he had just saved.

His sister had persuaded his pregnant, grief-stricken wife and family to flee with her to Syria but after only a short time, it became obvious they were not safe there either and so began the long journey through Turkey, across the sea to Greece, where they were kept in refugee camps with no sanitation and a lack of food and clothing. They existed from day to day, huddled together as if part of a huge cattle market. Their once happy, normal family life gone forever.

"I would like to paint a picture like that," Leila said, studying the painting intently. "They all look so happy in their beautiful garden. So at peace."

"Then you should," Miss Wells said encouragingly. "I'll arrange for someone to pose for you at the next art class."

Leila laughed softly. Her deep, dark eyes, usually so sad, lit up at the prospect. Looking at beautiful art eased the pain which was constantly present in her heart.

Joel was standing behind Leila; his gaze moving from her to the painting, which was obviously absorbing all her attention. He too felt, for a moment, that an invisible force was lifting his spirits, taking him somewhere beyond the mundane existence of everyday life.

He would love to bring his mother here to see such beauty but he knew that was unlikely to happen in her present state. Perhaps he'd make it a surprise on her birthday. He'd save some of the money from Jordan, just enough from the amount he handed over to his mother, to give her a special day.

"That you, Joel?" his mother called as she heard the front door close. There was anxiety in her voice. "Thank goodness you're back. Where've you been?" She looked blearily up at him as he entered the living room.

The television was blaring out so loudly he was surprised she hadn't had the neighbour banging on the thin walls. Perhaps she had, but in her present state Gemma would have simply ignored it.

She lay sprawled across the sofa in a cream, silk dressing gown, one of the few items of clothing she still possessed from her more affluent days. She obviously had not bothered to dress today. An empty gin bottle lay on the floor beside her, the threadbare rug dampened where the remaining drops of alcohol had spilt onto it. Beside the bottle was a glass ashtray piled high with cigarette butts.

"I told you, Mum, I was going to the National Gallery with the school."

He bent down and retrieved the bottle and ashtray, taking them to the bin by the sink where he discarded the empty bottle and threw in the cigarette butts, trying to ignore the nausea which suddenly invaded his senses from the acrid contents.

He had wanted her to ask how the visit was, so he could describe the beauty of the paintings, how awe-inspiring they were, how he felt the experience somehow changed his view of life, although he wasn't exactly sure in what way!

"I need you to go and collect something for me." Her voice was croaky and desperate.

His heart sank. He knew what that meant.

"My purse is over there." She pointed to the carved sideboard standing against one wall; its surface crammed with antique vases, china ornaments and framed photographs, mostly of Joel as a baby and then through various years at school. Any family photos featuring his father had been removed.

Joel had always admired this piece of furniture. There appeared to be a quality about it which stood apart from everything else in the flat. Perhaps it was because it was the one piece of furniture his mother had inherited from her parents before they fell out.

She was becoming more stressed. "Can you get a move on, Joel? I need my medication now!"

They both knew she was not referring to normal medication. Reluctantly, he took a twenty pound note and held it up.

"You'll need more than that... there's a couple of fifties in the back."

Joel reluctantly took the money; he hated it when his mother was like this

"Take those to the barber in the high street, next to Ali the greengrocer. He'll know what you've come for."

"Who will?" Joel stuffed the notes into the pocket of his rucksack. "Ali or the hairdresser?"

"The barber!" She grew more impatient and more desperate.

Joel strolled towards the front door. "See yer," he said grumpily, almost slamming the door behind him.

He could feel the tears start to prick his eyes as if someone was sticking pins into them. A salty teardrop slid down to his upper lip. He rubbed it away with the back of his hand.

"Boys don't cry."

All the happiness which had embraced his senses and lifted his mood at the gallery suddenly evaporated and he was thrown back into a world of doom and gloom, whose companions were darkness and depression.

He thought of Leila's silky, ebony hair falling down her slender back and of her enthusiasm for the paintings, gasping for joy as she discovered a new feature in each composition. Perhaps there was something in the life of an artist with which she could identify. Miss Wells had told them that many artists led impoverished lives and that van Gogh had never sold a painting in his lifetime, which seemed so unfair when today his canvases sold for millions at art auctions.

Leila had been through so much more than he had in her young life, Joel mused as he turned into the high street, glancing nervously around to make sure no one was following him. To have lost most of her family in such a cruel manner must have been so hard to bear and yet, perhaps because of her suffering, she seemed to be such a strong person.

He reached the barber's shop: a rather run-down building badly in need of a coat of paint on the exterior. However, peering through the misted window, there seemed to be quite a few clients inside, mostly portly men of various nationalities, some with tattooed-covered arms, having their beards trimmed.

Hesitantly, Joel put his hand on the door handle and stepped inside. The linoleum patterned floor was covered in clumps of hair, which a skinny, young boy of about twelve years old, whom Joel thought he recognised from the first year at school, attempted to sweep up with a brush which looked bigger than he was. An odour of body smells intermingled with stale smoke invaded the air.

Luckily, no one seemed to take any notice as Joel entered and approached a broad-shouldered man, whose own greying hair was tied into a ponytail. A sparkling earring adorned his left earlobe and he wore a bright, embroidered waistcoat over a shiny, black shirt. His jeans were extremely tight, Joel observed. The man was busily shaving the back of a client's bulbous, hairy neck.

Both men had noticed the reflection of Joel approaching in the mirror facing them. The ponytailed man briefly turned to look at him.

"You'll have to wait your turn, lad. I'm busy right now," he glowered.

"I'm not here for a haircut," Joel spoke quickly. "I need to see Eddie." He tried to sound as official as he could.

Immediately, the barber switched off the electric shaver. "I'm Eddie," he said gruffly. "Who sent you?"

The customer was obviously listening.

"My mum."

"Who's your mum?"

"Gemma Barnett." Joel shuffled from one foot to the other. He did not like this place or the man.

"Shit," the barber hissed under his breath, then addressing Joel said, "Go and sit over there, young man. I'll be with you as soon as I've finished with my customer here."

He leant forwards as he returned to shaving the man's neck, saying something in his ear as he did so.

He finished rather hurriedly and, removing the towel, apologised to his client, brushing the leftover hair onto the linoleum flooring and beckoning to the young lad to come and sweep it up.

Joel found himself sitting upon a chrome chair in a dark corner of the salon (if it could be described as a salon) and waited for Eddie to come over. Suddenly, he was standing in front of Joel.

"This way." He beckoned Joel to follow him into a dingy back room, full of hairdressing equipment and clutter: empty boxes, dirty coffee cups, an old fridge and a microwave surrounded by smelly, disused cartons of ready-made meals.

Eddie walked towards the microwave, taking a small parcel from inside. He turned back to Joel.

"Payment first," he demanded with an outstretched hand.

Joel hastily retrieved the two fifty pound notes from his rucksack and placed them in Eddie's solid palms.

Eddie didn't say a word as he took the money and handed the parcel to Joel.

"You make sure you take this straight to your mum, right?"

Joel nodded obediently.

"And tell her she owes me. It's only 'cause it's her I'm lettin' you 'ave it." He took out a cigarette and lit it, puffing as if his life depended on it. "Right, now beat it and tell your mum next time to come 'erself."

Joel was about to say she was incapable of going anywhere and all because of people like Eddie but thought better of it. He was a lot bigger than Joel and looked as if he was prone to violent mood swings.

Eddie ushered Joel out of a side door so he did not have to re-enter the shop and Joel marched as fast as he could down the high street, heading back to his estate.

Autumn was closing in and the nights were getting shorter. He knew many of his school friends carried knives as he did, but he dreaded ever having to use it, particularly on dark evenings such as this when anything or anyone could suddenly leap out from behind the shadows.

A group of older teenagers were huddled in a corner near the lifts; hoods pulled over their heads and puffing on illegal substances: crack, coke, weed.

A week earlier, a boy, not much older than Joel, had died from inhaling a substance acquired from an unreliable source. Such a waste of life. Joel wondered whether the perpetrators of this crime ever felt any remorse for causing the death of another human being. He knew the lure of money was a tempting seductress and many of these boys had never known love and compassion, themselves being starved of any affection from the day they were born, some even abused by the very people who brought them into the world.

Joel grunted a greeting to the teenagers as he pressed the button to call the lift. He felt a sense of relief that he was the only person travelling in it, despite the usual stench of unpleasant odours, but as soon as it rattled to a halt, he had the usual sense of dread about what sort of condition he would find his mother in when he walked through the door.

She seemed to have made a partial recovery, however. She was wearing one of her best dresses, had brushed her hair and applied make-up to her usually pale face. She even smiled warmly when Joel walked in.

"Did you get it?" she asked quickly.

Joel handed her the package; he wished she could feel his disgust.

"He told me to say never send anyone else again. You must go yourself."

"Oh?" She almost snatched the package from his hand. "Take no notice of him. He'd soon change his mind if I stopped being a customer."

Joel assumed she wasn't talking about hair appointments.

"Why are you all dressed up?" he asked, removing his rucksack from his back and taking off his jacket. "You've made a quick recovery."

Gemma blushed. "Ah, yes, well…" She paused. "An old friend of mine called round, completely out of the blue. He's been away on a world tour, a musician and old friend of your father's."

Joel's heart sank at the mention of his father. He immediately dismissed from his mind what might have been. He would have liked to ask whether this "friend" ever saw his father or knew whether he still lived in this country or had moved abroad. However, he knew that in his mother's head, his father no longer existed and he would never dare to mention his name in her presence. He could sympathise with the pain which his father had caused her and yet the older he grew, he felt that to offer forgiveness was surely preferable to a life of hate and resentment. He would have dearly loved to see his father and wondered whether his father ever felt the same. He thought of Leila, who adored her father. He had been cruelly taken away from her and she had no chance of ever seeing him again as he was no longer alive.

"So?" Joel said sullenly.

"He persuaded me to get dressed and go out for a drink in town. He's picking me up soon. I won't be late back." She picked up a new packet of cigarettes from the kitchen table and dropped them into her designer handbag, one of the few gifts from his father which she had not thrown out. "You'll be all right, love, won't you? There's a pizza in the fridge. Your favourite."

Joel stood in silent thought, trying to decide whether he preferred his mother "out of her head" or going on a date with a man and wondering how trustworthy he was.

He did not have to wait long to be re-assured as the doorbell rang and an excited Gemma gestured to him to go and answer it.

Tony Millbank was tall, above average height, with a face which, despite engraved with wrinkles, was still handsome. His greying hair rested upon his broad shoulders and his deep green eyes complemented his seductive smile. He wore an open-neck aquamarine-coloured shirt, blue jeans and a grey, crushed velvet jacket. When he spoke, it was with a cultured accent, just as Joel's mother had once possessed and traces of it still remained.

"Hi." He smiled broadly at Joel. "You must be Joel."

He held out his hand and Joel shook it. His grasp was strong. Always, as Joel's granny used to say, a good sign of character.

Granny also said that you could tell a man by the style and state of his shoes. Joel wasn't so sure about that judging from his mates, but then there weren't trainers in Granny's day!

Tony turned to Gemma. "You look fantastic."

He took her in outstretched arms and embraced her affectionately; his lips brushing her left cheek lightly.

In that moment, Joel realised it had been a long time since his mother had received any affection from a man, apart from Joel himself, of course.

Gemma thanked him for the compliment.

"Is it okay with you, young man, if I take your mother out for a bite to eat?"

Joel nodded. What else was he expected to say, although he was pleased for his mother.

"We won't be late back." His mother kissed him on the cheek as she swept passed, hand-in-hand with Tony, towards the front door.

Joel ran to the window and peered at the street below which bordered the estate, curious to see what sort of car Tony drove. His eyes followed them as they walked like a pair of young lovers along the pavement, where a few of the local residents stood watching.

Then, to his amazement, Joel saw a chauffeur leap out of a black Mercedes and open the doors to usher them inside. It was a life he presumed his mother could have led, had she not been seduced by the roadie instead of a member of the band.

Joel turned away and went to the fridge, opening the door and seeing the frozen pizza his mother had spoken of. He decided he really wasn't that hungry. He picked up his phone checking for messages and walked towards the couch where his eyes fell upon the package he had delivered to his mother earlier. He was daring himself to open it, perhaps even try some of its contents, to discover what was so alluring about these substances which had the power to seduce and destroy the lives of so many people. He stared at it for several minutes, wondering whether such a decision could change his life forever.

At that moment, his mobile beeped with a text from Leila.

Hello, how are you? I really enjoyed today at the gallery. Did you?

For a brief moment, Joel experienced a surge of happiness; someone who shared his feelings about the art they had both seen for the first time. Proof that human beings were capable of creating great things which could inspire and transport the human imagination into a world beyond everyday reality.

Without hesitation, he texted his reply.

It was mind-blowing.

He half-heartedly ate the pizza, which upon second thoughts, he had placed in the microwave. His previously negative mood was replaced by a sense of being alive and it was Leila who had given him this gift.

Perhaps we should go to a gallery together sometime? she replied.

Yes, I would like that.

Me too. Goodnight.

Joel decided not to wait up for his mother to return. She had said she would not be late but he had heard that many times before.

He went to bed and fell easily into a deep sleep. Perhaps, he had mused before falling asleep, there was hope for a better future and a way out of the endless circle of drugs, money and fear for the future, which seemed to hang over him like a dark foreboding cloud, threatening an eternal storm of destruction.

Tony had taken Gemma to a fashionable West End restaurant, followed by a visit to his Mayfair club where she had drunk too much champagne and danced the night away. It had been a long time since she had felt so liberated and free to enjoy herself. She still turned heads upon entering a room with her sophisticated model looks, which Joel's father used to compare to a well-bred and highly strung racehorse.

Tony led her onto the dancefloor as the DJ played Chris de Burgh's "Lady in Red", which was appropriate as Gemma had chosen her favourite red silk dress to wear. As he held her close, she nestled her head against his shoulder, enjoying the sensation of having another body pressed against hers, whilst his strong arms enveloped her protectively.

Tony's chauffeur drove them back to the estate in the early hours of the morning where Tony insisted upon accompanying Gemma to her door. He had forgotten how some people

were forced to combat such Dickensian conditions in twenty-first century Britain.

"Thank you for a wonderful evening." Gemma fell against his shoulder as they stood outside the front door. She suddenly felt ashamed of the shabbiness of where she lived.

Tony kissed her affectionately upon the cheek. "It was great to see you, Gem. Glad you enjoyed it." He turned to go. "I'll be in touch."

During the following weeks, Joel noticed his mother was a different person. It was as if Tony had awakened her from the dead, like some handsome prince in those soppy fairy tales she used to read to Joel as a toddler!

CHAPTER FOUR

Joel was still a runner for Jordan and still earning good money, which he gave to his mother and suspected she still gave to her dealer, but she also seemed to spend some of it on a new wardrobe and no longer lounged around all day in dressing gowns.

Joel was elated to see this new glamorous mother and also looked forward to seeing Tony, who obviously was responsible for her transformation. They no longer always went out to eat at smart restaurants. Instead, Tony would ask his chauffeur to collect meals already prepared, which the three of them would share amidst convivial conversation, interspersed with laughter. Something which seemed to have been missing from their lives for some time.

Knowing his mother was no longer alone and appeared to be in good hands, Joel had been spending more time with Leila and upon one occasion, she had invited him home to meet her mother, sister and brother, who had been a baby when their father had been killed. Their aunt, who had fled Syria with them, had found employment in the north of England and no longer lived with them.

The council had housed them in a depressing period property, where fungi grew upon the damp walls, protruding silently like a slithering snake from beneath the peeling pre-war wallpaper. The embossed paper once had depicted scenes of prancing peacocks strutting amidst exotic shrubs. That was during the days when the now almost derelict Victorian house would have been occupied by a professional middle-class family, who would have entertained in style.

Now, the once grand house had been converted into twelve "apologies" for apartments and Leila and her family occupied two high-ceilinged and draughty rooms.

In one, there were two single beds pushed together where the children slept, whilst their mother had constructed a creation made of wooden planks and chairs, resembling those which the ancient Egyptians used to sleep upon. She had placed a plank of wood somewhat precariously between two dining chairs. The chairs enabled her to place the plank several inches above the cold linoleum floor as she was afraid of the mice, which frequently scuttled across the room in the darkness of the night and the cockroaches crawling creepily across her face as she slept.

They shared a bathroom and toilet with three other families, all asylum seekers, who, having suffered so much in order to reach the "promised land" after a perilous journey halfway across the world, found themselves existing in conditions, which were little better than those they had left behind.

Being mostly male, it was usually left to Leila's mother to clean the communal toilet, which she attempted to do, eventually becoming exasperated as no one else ever did and she would complain she was sick and tired of clearing up other people's "shit".

Leila told Joel that, at home, when she was younger, their mother had always been so house proud and kept the house clean and immaculate for her husband and children.

"Do you miss your home?" Joel asked one evening as he and Leila sat upon a bench on the common munching Maltesers, whilst a hopeful pigeon circled expectantly above their heads.

"I miss how my life there was," Leila replied, "And, of course, I miss my father every day and my big sisters and cousins and friends but I would not recognise the city now. So much has been destroyed. All the beautiful historical buildings which stood for thousands of years have been reduced to rubble by the bombings."

Joel regretted having asked the question, seeing the sad expression which cast itself, like a dark shadow, across her pretty face.

However bad life had been for him, with his father in prison and his mother turning to drink and drugs and he himself having no choice but to be a runner for a drug gang, none of it was as traumatic as the suffering which Leila and her family had endured. He imagined his own flat. No palace, it was true, but he always felt safe there. He could not imagine how he would react if it were suddenly destroyed in a bomb attack or invaded by men with machetes in their hands and hate in their hearts. He dreaded to think how he would have survived such an horrendous situation.

Joel wondered why the human race seemed incapable of living together in harmony. Instead, people continually chose to fight and destroy each other. Even in his own situation, he wished his time at school could be positive rather than negative and that all his classmates could be friends rather than potential enemies.

They had finished the packet of Maltesers apart from a single chocolate ball left in the packet.

"You have it." Joel offered her the packet.

She smiled and gave him a sideways glance; her raven hair and velvet brown eyes looking up at him from beneath the brightly coloured scarf which partially covered her head.

Leila often wore pretty scarves but she did not wear a hijab as the Yazidi religion did not stipulate that one should.

"I was going to ask if you'd like to come and eat with us at home one evening," he blurted out, afraid in case she refused.

"I'd like that very much," she said as they stood up and, saying goodbye, walked off in separate directions. Leila quickened her pace, knowing her mother always worried until the moment Leila walked through the door.

Joel had already told Gemma and Tony about Leila and the traumas she and her family had suffered. They both agreed that, of course, she would be more than welcome. Gemma suggested Joel invite the whole family but he was not as keen on that idea. Perhaps at a later date. But for now, he would like to get to know Leila better.

"What is Leila's favourite food?" Tony asked, already planning the menu.

Joel realised he didn't have a clue!

The following day in the break between history and English, Joel tapped Leila on the shoulder and quietly, almost conspiratorially, asked what her favourite meal was.

Leila smiled. "My really favourite food was a dish my mother used to make back home but you do not have such food in this country, so my favourite meal here is fish and chips."

Joel laughed. "Are you serious?"

"Yes." She nodded enthusiastically. "Once a month, my mother saves enough money from her cleaning jobs to buy us all fish and chips on a Friday. It is delicious."

Tony laughed when Joel relayed this conversation to him.

"Well, fish and chips it is then. But…" He paused, his grey-green eyes narrowing into a frown as if in deep contemplation. "I have an idea. Leila says she cannot get her favourite food from back home in this country, but I'm not so sure. Let me make some enquiries."

Joel never ceased to be amazed by the way Tony's brain worked. Not only was he always full of ideas and problem solving but he seemed to get a real joy from making people happy. The way Gemma had changed since Tony's arrival upon the scene was a perfect example. Tony himself always said that Lady Luck had been good to him and he wanted to share his good luck with others.

✦ ✦ ✦

Friday night arrived and Joel waited patiently at the school gates for Leila. He was unaware of the prying eyes of Jordan, who had noticed lately how well Joel and the Yazidi girl were getting on. Jordan admitted it was true that she was very attractive with her dark, mysterious looks but he had heard it said that the more of her sort we took into this country, the worse it was for us. You couldn't trust foreigners, especially her type and Britain was already at breaking point. Like a ship where the captain lets passengers pile on until the weight is too much for the structure of the ship and it sinks to the bottom of the ocean.

"Waiting for your fancy bitch?" Jordan took Joel by surprise, appearing at his side.

At the same moment, Leila strode towards them, carrying a rucksack heavy with books.

"Hi," she greeted them both cheerily.

"What a touching sight," Jordan almost spat sarcastically. "Off to have a bit of fun, are we?"

"Leila's coming to supper," Joel said, swiftly moving protectively in front of the young girl. "In fact, we have to go or we'll be late." He ushered Leila away from the school gates.

"Right fucking little gentleman, aren't we?" Jordan sneered. "Just don't forget who you take your orders from.

I may well need you tonight, so keep your mobile switched on."

Joel felt sick in the pit of his stomach. Having Jordan always on his back made him feel like a prisoner whose life was not his own; his every move was registered and he was Jordan's puppet to play with as he pleased. More to the point, Joel could see no way of being released from his captor's clutches.

There was a delicious aroma of cooking when Joel and Leila entered the flat, which was in stark contrast to the foul smells in the lift which they had just taken.

Gemma sat on the sofa drinking a glass of wine and Tony sat beside her. Joel thought how pretty his mother looked. The light from the Chinese table lamp nearby seemed to enhance her youthful appearance and her wavy fair hair framed her immaculately made-up face.

Tony, who always looked smart, even when dressed casually, was wearing chinos and a purple silk shirt.

"Mum, Tony…" Joel hesitated as they both stood up. "This is Leila."

They took Leila's hand enthusiastically.

"So pleased to meet you, Leila," Tony's deep voice boomed. "We've heard so much about you."

Joel cringed inwardly. Why did adults always have to be so embarrassing?

Leila smiled sweetly, if slightly embarrassed.

"Hello," she said quietly.

"Smells good," Joel said enthusiastically, hoping no more would be said about him talking about his guest.

"Well," Tony said, "I hope you like it, Leila. It won't be exactly what you used to have in your country, but I think it may be pretty close."

Leila looked puzzled. "I thought Joel said we were having fish and chips." She turned to glance at Joel.

"Well," Tony said, "You can have fish and chips any time. The next time you come, if you like, but we wanted this to be a special surprise."

"I'm sure it will be delicious," Leila said politely.

"I'll just put my stuff in my bedroom." Joel headed across the room.

"Well, Leila, shall we sit down?" Gemma gestured towards the dining table, which had been set beautifully with a silky cream table cloth and shining cutlery and glasses.

Tony had researched the type of food which Leila would have been used to back home and had hired a chef to cook delicious lamb and chicken stews with lots of tomato sauce, rice, breads, cheeses, honey and yoghurts.

As the food was served, a look of delight spread across Leila's face. The table resembled a subject for a still life painting with such an assortment of colourful dishes: stuffed grape leaves, kulicha, cream, nuts, cinnamon, pistachios, golden syrups...

"Please help yourselves," Tony instructed.

"This looks wonderful."

As Leila savoured the feast laid before her, her eyes fell upon her favourite dish. Kibbeh was a mixture of bulgur wheat, minced onions, spices and ground meat. Leila wondered whether it would taste as good as when her mother made it. Gemma gestured to Joel to pass Leila the dish and as she took a mouthful, she had to admit it was every bit as delicious.

Tony took great pleasure in observing Leila's reaction as she tasted each dish. He tried to imagine what she had been through in her short life but did not want to pry or upset her by reviving painful memories.

It was Leila, however, who began to speak about the life she had led before fleeing her war-torn country.

"The last time I saw such a feast was my cousin's wedding back home," she said shyly. "The whole family and guests sat on a beautiful, enormous carpet and were served many different dishes and afterwards, musicians came and entertained us with ancient Yazidi songs and played the tambur and other native instruments. Dancing girls used their colourful silk scarves to create shapes around them, as if the scarves were also dancing."

She laughed and Joel realised he rarely heard her laugh.

"I'd be very interested to hear your native music," Tony said.

"It is very beautiful and haunting," Leila replied, "But I don't know where you would find anyone here who could perform it for you."

"Well…" Tony was thoughtful. "Perhaps you could give me a demonstration some time, if you'd like to. I'm sure you must remember some of the songs."

Leila bowed her head coyly. "Oh, perhaps. I will have to try to remember."

"Well, yes, think about it and let me know when you feel ready. I have a recording studio so we could do something there."

"Hey, Leila," Joel said enthusiastically, "Tony could make you a pop star."

Leila looked alarmed and Tony reassured her. "We'll just record something which your mother might like to hear. What do you think?"

Leila nodded. "It is her birthday soon and I would like that very much. She used to sing a lot around the house and had a lovey voice before…" She hesitated. "Before IS came."

"Right, well, let's see what we can do. You can let Joel know when is a good time for you."

"Yes, I will do. Thank you." Leila smiled. "I do remember a song my grandparents, who lived in the countryside, used to sing. I loved going to stay with them and helping to milk the goats. I even had my own pony. Some nights, in the summer, we were allowed to sleep in tents and that was when the grown-ups would sing and the children would dance as my grandfather played the tambur and some of his helpers played drums."

"It sounds blissful," Gemma said. "I always wanted to see those faraway lands and now I don't suppose I ever will. Are your grandparents still alive?"

Leila continued. Her words flowed almost like a river which had burst its banks, as if she had wanted to tell this story for a very long time but had never had the opportunity.

"The grandparents in the country died of old age which my mother said she was happy about as they missed the destruction which followed. My father's parents had a house in the medina where my grandfather had once sold carpets to kings, sultans, princes and potentates from all over the world. When ISIL came, they forbade the sale of luxury goods so my grandfather had to close his business. When our house was bombed and my elder brothers and cousins who were visiting were killed, my mother and my younger sisters and baby brother went to live with my father's parents in Iraq.

"My father, fortunately, was working in the hospital trying to save people's lives the night our home was bombed but then two days later, the hospital was bombed. My father had just successfully operated upon a mother who, on her way to the hospital, had been badly wounded when a suicide bomber destroyed the marketplace as she was passing through it. My father operated upon the mother and her baby and saved them both but then more bombing started and, refusing to leave his patients, he stayed with them in the operating theatre where they all perished."

Joel glanced across at his mother and Tony who were visibly moved. Gemma wiped a tear away from her eye.

"How terribly tragic for you all." Gemma lit a cigarette, a habit which Tony had not managed to cure her of yet. "I'm so sorry."

"My grandparents and my aunt told my mother she must take us and flee to safety from Iraq. If we stayed, we would surely lose our lives too. My mother did not want to leave them but knew, for our sakes, she must. Daesh were also taking young girls like me and making them sex slaves. It happened to my best friend. She was beautiful and one day they entered her house and dragged her away and did terrible things to her. I never saw her again."

"So, where did you go to?" Joel asked.

"We went at first to Syria but that was not safe either. Every night, bombs exploded everywhere. My aunt came to join us and gave us an envelope full of money, which my grandfather had said we must use to get to safety. He had also arranged for a man to take us to safety.

"We left in the middle of the night. My grandfather had paid the man to smuggle us out in his cattle truck. He took us across the desert and then left us. We didn't know where we were and walked for miles and miles in the heat until we arrived at a refugee camp where the people running it welcomed us and were kind. But there were too many people crammed into small spaces and it was dirty and there were no toilets, just holes in the ground which stank. A lot of people became very sick.

"The day after we left, my grandparents' house was bombed and my grandmother was killed. My grandfather, as if by a miracle, survived, only to be taken outside with his neighbours, put against a wall and shot." The tears began to trickle down Leila's face.

Gemma stood up and went to put her arms around her. "You poor darling," she whispered.

"Shall I walk you home?" Joel asked protectively. He had wanted this to be a happy evening and now Leila was feeling sad.

"Thank you. Yes, Joel, I should be going."

"I'm so sorry," Tony said standing up. "We didn't mean to upset you."

"No, really, you haven't. It is good to remember those we loved. I hope more people in countries like this know what cruel things some evil people do, then perhaps one day there will be no more fighting and people can live in peace."

Gemma thought how wise Leila sounded for her years. She also thought of the drug wars and the young people senselessly stabbing each other to death only a short distance away from where she and Joel lived. She would never make sense of the world. It also occurred to her that she, in her own small way, was contributing to enabling the evil drug trade to flourish.

"Thank you again for such a delicious meal," Leila said as Joel led her towards the door.

"Our pleasure." Tony smiled, standing up.

Joel fetched his jacket and the colourful, embroidered shawl which Leila had worn when they arrived. A coolness had invaded the night air as they walked back across the estate and onto the common.

"I'm sorry they upset you," Joel said as they turned into the road where Leila lived.

"It was fine, really," Leila insisted. "Your mother and Tony are very kind people."

He said goodnight and Leila stepped inside the dilapidated building, knowing her mother would be anxiously waiting up for her. However, she was looking forward to seeing her mother's face light up when she presented her with the leftovers from the meal she had just enjoyed.

CHAPTER FIVE

"Eh, got a job for you tonight." Jordan accosted Joel the next day at school. "Keep your eye on your deal line," he ordered, referring to Joel's mobile.

Joel was becoming familiar with the language of the dealers or peddlers. He knew he was referred to as "Bic", which meant he was disposable, along with the numerous other young boys who had been forced into serving these evil characters as their slaves.

"How was your bitch?" Jordan's lips parted in a sarcastic sneer.

Joel wondered what Jordan's home life was like. He had heard that his mother had given up on him, unable to control him after his father had been killed. For that one moment, he thought they had almost seemed close when they had spoken about their fathers.

"Leila came to dinner, that was all."

"Leila came to dinner..." Jordan mimicked. "All posh, are we? And what was on the menu?"

Joel ignored this last remark and fortunately the bell rang for the next lesson. It was history but Joel was unable to concentrate with Jordan sitting behind him and muttering under his breath.

"What's wrong?" Leila asked at break time, noticing Joel's mournful expression.

"Oh, nothing, Leila. Just something I have to sort out."

He wanted to confess everything to Leila, to pour out his heart and tell her how he had become embroiled in this dreadful, evil world of drugs but it was not fair to burden her with his problems. She had suffered enough already.

In the art studio, the teacher, Eleanor Wells, was preparing the afternoon's lesson for her students. Friday afternoon's art lesson was always popular as it was a time when students could relax and attempt, whether good or bad, to be creative. They knew Miss Wells would encourage them all equally, whatever their ability to draw or paint.

Eleanor enjoyed teaching. She had taken the job in the first place as a stop gap before deciding what she wanted to do with her life. She knew she wanted to explore the world and would have moved permanently to another country but she knew that her parents, although they would never discourage her, would really miss their only daughter, who visited them at least once a month. However, if anyone had told her that ten years later, she would still be teaching art at the South London comprehensive, she would never have believed them.

At art school, she had dreamt of becoming a professional artist, not in the league of Picasso, Matisse and other great names, but at least producing paintings which people wished to hang in their homes. Her tutors praised her capability and encouraged her to always aim for the moon, as Oscar Wilde famously said, "Even if you miss, you'll land amongst the stars."

At the end of her second year, however, a young, handsome, out of work actor, who came to pose for life drawing classes, was to change the future she had planned.

Tom Morgan possessed a perfect body and undeniably handsome face and he knew it. He was also extremely vain and used to ask the students for all their sketches of him at the end of a session. As Eleanor was later to discover, he framed these sketches and hung them upon every available space in his Notting Hill flat.

Tom was not yet rich but neither was he poor. His father owned an estate agency in Hampstead and it was during the period when property prices were booming. Privately educated and accepted at RADA, Tom was expected to excel at his profession but at the time Eleanor knew him, it was mainly minor theatre parts, the odd TV series and commercial. He was not yet in the super rich bracket which a few privileged and sometimes talented actors reach.

"You don't do this for the money, do you?" Eleanor surprised herself with her directness as she and Tom shared a pizza and bottle of wine at an Italian bistro near the art school.

It was a warm and sunny spring day and Tom had suggested they go for a drink and a bite to eat. She wasn't expecting the invitation but saw no reason not to accept. She was also curious to know more about him. Fortunately, they were able to sit at an outside table, as Tom was a smoker, and enjoy the sunshine.

Eleanor was not sure why he had decided to choose her as his lunch companion. Quite a few of the female students were hoping he might notice them. His pale blue eyes pierced into hers. Eleanor silently likened his look to a laser beam emitted from a character in a science fiction film character.

"How perceptive of you!"

"Sorry, I didn't mean to be rude. I just know it pays peanuts and judging by your designer clothes..." She paused, conscious that the words were coming out all the wrong way. Hastily, she finished with, "I just wondered why you did it, that was all." She gulped down her second glass of wine, blushing with embarrassment.

Tom finished his pizza and, taking a cigarette from his packet, lit it, holding it momentarily pursed between his lips.

"I think you know the reason why I model for your life class."

He drew upon the cigarette and a puff of smoke circled in the air above them. Eleanor recalled the smoke rings as signals sent by native Americans to warn each other of the danger of approaching cowboys.

She had loved the cowboy movies which she watched on television with her father as a child. A strange choice of programmes for a gentle vicar perhaps, although father and daughter enjoyed watching good conquer evil when the baddies were captured by the goodies.

"Oh?" She sipped the third glass of wine which he had poured for her. She knew this would go to her head.

"Don't play the innocent with me, young lady." She was nineteen and he was twenty-eight. "I admit I'm a vain creature and you know that too."

Eleanor smiled. "Okay, I admit it." She finished her wine, she had encountered a real life Narcissus, the hunter in Greek myths who fell in love with his own reflection in a pond.

"Would you like to see my flat? Then you can judge for yourself how vain I am."

"All right." She was definitely beginning to feel a little light-headed and probably it would have been wiser to decline his invitation.

She gathered her bags and searched for her purse but he clamped his hand over hers.

"My treat, I insist."

"Well, in that case, thank you," Eleanor said and was genuinely grateful for his generosity as her bank account was permanently in the red.

Tom unexpectedly took her hand as they walked towards the tube station. His flat was in Notting Hill, which was a few stops along the line.

He lived on the middle floor of a large imposing, Edwardian house, which stood alongside similar houses in the wide street.

After climbing the once grand staircase, they reached the door to his apartment, which he unlocked, gesturing to Eleanor to enter before him being the perfect gentleman he was. The small hallway led into a high-ceilinged sitting room with floor to ceiling windows, through which the strong sunlight shone across the off-white walls and cream carpet, illuminating shimmering dancing dust specks in the air.

The furniture was minimalist but displayed good taste: white sofas, expensive glass topped coffee tables, Anglepoise metallic lighting, elegant side tables in shades of greys and oatmeal. The only splashes of colour were supplied by the Moroccan cashmere throws and cushions.

As she surveyed the room, Eleanor's eyes fell upon the pictures, tastefully framed and hung in sequence along the walls; they were in charcoal and pencil and all the work of her fellow students. Eleanor had to admit they were of a high standard and did look impressive.

"Good talking point," Tom remarked, watching her reaction.

"They fit well in here."

"Oh, there are more in the bedroom, bathroom, loo..."

He took her hand playfully and led her across the room and into the bedroom. Again, high-ceilinged and elegant as one would expect.

Eleanor had never seen such a huge bed. A family of five could easily fit into it, she thought. Again, the framed drawings of Tom were hanging on every surrounding wall, resembling a shrine to some saint, reminding Eleanor of her visits to Catholic churches in France and Italy where women would genuflect to religious statues positioned around the ornate interiors.

She felt a sense of calm in this room and therefore was not prepared for what happened next. As she stood admiring the room and the colourful Mexican quilted bedspread, a work of art in itself and no doubt created by local villagers somewhere in the Mexican countryside, she was aware of Tom standing behind her, so close that she could feel his warm breath upon her neck.

He stepped towards the bed, pulling back the bedspread and folding it carefully, before placing it upon an elegant French antique sofa positioned beneath the window. This was the only antique piece of furniture in the room but fitted in with the contemporary pieces perfectly. Eleanor imagined how many ancient French posteriors had been seated upon its golden satin upholstery. Perhaps even Louis XIV himself or one of his mistresses.

Turning back towards the bed, Tom smiled across at Eleanor. Her bare feet were sinking into the thick piled carpet. Tom had asked her to remove her shoes, as he himself had done, upon entering the flat.

Suddenly and without warning, Tom clasped her arms and pulled her down onto the bed, where she lay motionless upon the white Egyptian cotton sheets. At first, she was speechless from shock but then she felt the weight of his body upon her and realised he was already half-undressed.

She attempted to wriggle from beneath him and protested loudly, "Tom, stop, what on earth do you think you're doing?"

He merely smiled, his face looking down upon hers. "Come on, darling, you're not that naive." He threw his discarded chinos onto the floor and Eleanor realised he wasn't wearing any underpants.

He lowered himself onto her and his look was almost one of tenderness.

"Don't tell me you haven't desired my body ever since I started posing for your life classes." The tone of his voice was seductive. "Just think, you can tell all your female classmates how I chose you and watch them squirm with envy."

Eleanor's instinct was to sit up, push him aside and make an escape. She could not believe the arrogance of the man but he was too strong for her slight physique and had her pinned to the bed.

He had begun unbuttoning her blouse, pushing up her bra, pinching her erect nipples.

Eleanor had no strength to fight the powerful pressure of his body, beneath which she lay like a lamb to the slaughter.

If she were honest, she was beginning to find it hard to resist his sensuous masculinity and the light-headedness brought on by the wine only encouraged her passivity as she lay prostrate like a helpless nymph before her Bacchus.

His lips briefly brushed against hers but he was more intent upon entering her. She was totally unprepared for the pain she experienced at first (she had no chance to tell him she was the virgin daughter of a vicar), but this gave way to the pleasant sensation of his moving back and forth inside her. However, as his penetration became deeper and his thrusts quickened, she could not supress a cry of pain. Instead of becoming gentler, this seemed to excite him even more.

"Harder, harder, you beautiful bitch," he shouted, as with one final thrust and a cry almost of strangulation, it was all over and he withdrew from her as quickly as he had entered, leaving Eleanor confused, unsatisfied, and suffering from both shame and sadness.

Tom rolled over nonchalantly, took a cigarette from the packet lying on the marble topped bedside table and lit it. He offered her a drag, which she refused, turning her head away. He showed no concern for how she might be feeling.

She rolled off the bed and retrieved her clothes. Looking back at his naked body, she realised he had fallen asleep.

Quietly, she tiptoed across the bedroom floor, across the sitting room and, putting on her shoes, left through the front door.

Outside in the spring air again, she took a deep breath, reflecting how her life had changed in such a short time. During the course of just one afternoon.

Walking back past the bistro, where a few hours earlier she and Tom had enjoyed such a pleasant lunch, she remembered how happy she had felt. Now, barely an hour later, she felt completely deflated and angry with herself for behaving so naively.

She took the tube back to the tiny flat she rented above the local bakery in West Hampstead and made herself a strong coffee, before going into the bathroom, throwing off her clothes and stepping into a steaming hot bath.

Soaking in the soapy water, the memories of the afternoon flashed through her mind like unwelcome visions from a horror movie. How could something which should have been so sensual and memorable become no more than a depressing and degrading experience?

She knew she would never be able to draw his body again and would ask to move to another life drawing class. The models in her new class were all female and Eleanor felt more comfortable with this.

Fortunately, she managed to avoid bumping into Tom over the next few weeks. Occasionally, there was a faint hope that he might get in touch, apologise for his ungallant behaviour and beg her forgiveness, perhaps even declaring his undying love! However, she heard nothing at all and chided herself for even harbouring such thoughts.

At first, Eleanor had attempted to wipe the episode from her memory just as she might paint over a canvas and start again, but instead of time healing, her thoughts kept returning to that fateful afternoon in Tom's immaculate flat.

As a young girl, she had dreamt of a handsome man making mad, passionate love to her, whispering poetic words in her ear and giving her a romantic experience which she would remember forever.

At home, one or two local boys had unbuttoned her blouse and nervously fondled her pubescent breasts. Another took her home when his parents were out, and persuaded her to lie on the Persian rug in front of the fireplace for a cuddle, then began stroking her leg, moving his hand up to her thigh and pushing it inside her knickers, which she had to confess she quite enjoyed. Fortunately, at that point, the parents had returned home early and there was a great deal of scrambling off the floor and straightening of clothes.

However, all the boys Eleanor knew were polite, their parents knew each other and none of them would have dreamt of forcing themselves upon her.

Eleanor was still troubled by the fact that Tom had excited her and aroused new sensations and emotions within her, which she convinced herself was the only explanation she could find for not fighting him off more forcefully. After the initial pain of forcing himself inside her, there was a brief moment of pleasure but when he began hurting her, it was obvious he was only satisfying his own urges and desires. No doubt Tom had assumed it wasn't the first time for her but she knew he would have known the truth when he awoke and saw the specks of blood upon his spotless white sheet.

Eleanor did find relief in her painting and her tutor congratulated her upon how much more mature her compositions were.

She decided to put the experience behind her and concentrate upon her future. She had made friends with a group of fellow students, two male and three female, whose company she enjoyed and whose sense of humour she shared.

There was one in particular, George, a slim fair-haired, fine featured young man who was recovering from a homosexual affair and who poured his heart out to Eleanor over endless cups of Earl Grey tea and cappuccinos, which they drank in a small café nearby to the art school. The owner was Polish but adored western pop music and there was always the Beatles, Rod Stewart, the Rolling Stones or Bowie playing in the background. Eleanor and her friends were more into Oasis, Robbie Williams and Nirvana. They were always trying to persuade her to go to various music festivals with them at weekends. Although she enjoyed the music, she had no desire to go and stand for hours on end, surrounded by a mass of humanity, in order to listen to a band live. She realised that for many it was a rewarding and enjoyable experience, no doubt heightened with various types of drugs, which she knew many of them indulged in.

She wasn't being particularly moral about this. If she was honest, Justin, an old friend from home who was studying at London University, had turned up quite unexpectedly on her doorstep one day and, being both pleased and surprised to see him, she had invited him in and shared her supper of chicken casserole. After they had eaten and were relaxing in her tiny crimson painted sitting room, he had suggested they smoke cannabis together and not wanting to appear a strait-laced goodie two shoes, she had joined him in puffing on a "spliff", as he called it, which he had carefully rolled for them to share.

Immediately after taking a couple of puffs, Eleanor had felt very peculiar and disoriented as her heart began beating at an alarming rate. She excused herself and said she needed to go to the bathroom.

Her surroundings were spinning around and she could feel herself drifting into a strange and unfamiliar place. Lying down upon the bathroom floor, she was sure she was going to lose consciousness. She felt she was floating in space and looking down from the ceiling at her own body. She was terrified and had visions of her parents, who might never see her again. Not only was she drifting in and out of a plethora of strange and frightening experiences, both in mind and body, she was completely out of control and terrified.

When she eventually returned to reality, she was relieved to still be alive, vowing never to touch drugs again. The old school friend, meanwhile, was blissfully unaware of what she had been through. With a contented smile upon his face, he was still lying upon her old couch, which Eleanor had covered with a gaily patterned piece of old curtain. The material had dramatically become a living tropical forest under the effect of the spliff. She told Justin that she really did not feel well and that he should leave as she was going straight to bed.

"Oh." His voice was full of disappointment. "But I thought we could make mad, passionate love together." He walked towards her with his arms outstretched.

Eleanor tried to remain patient but, in reality, was trying to control her anger.

"I think you should go," she insisted and showed him to the door, shutting it firmly behind him.

In actual fact she felt too afraid to go to sleep in case she didn't wake up. She knew so many of her friends took recreational drugs and thought nothing of it. She also knew there was a big cocaine problem amongst professional people. She was aware that, in the past, cocaine became very fashionable amongst aristocrats, who had enjoyed cocaine-fuelled parties. She remembered her father telling her that he had once been administered cocaine by his dentist as an anaesthetic but he had not given any details of its effect.

Eleanor often wondered whether she could confide in George about her sexual episode with Tom but decided to say nothing, at least for the time being. She also knew George had fancied Tom when he was in the life class for which Tom posed, so she felt it probably better not to mention it.

Two months later, however, she had no one to whom she could turn but George when a pregnancy test from the chemist showed positive. Term had ended for the summer holiday and her girlfriends had either returned to their parents' homes in various parts of the country or, those who could afford it, were taking a break abroad. She and George were the only two of their group who remained in London as both of them had found part-time work for the summer and they needed the money. Eleanor was fond of her parents but really had no desire to spend the summer months at the vicarage in the Herefordshire village, helping her mother with afternoon teas for the Women's Institute. She knew they would be disappointed but they would understand she needed to earn some money in order to pay her rent. She would visit them for the occasional weekend.

Eleanor had also begun to paint whenever she had the chance, encouraged by her tutor, who was sure she had every chance of becoming a professional and successful artist.

After examining the pregnancy test at home, however, she knew her life would change forever. She would have to tell her parents, who would, as Christians, be understanding but disappointed in their talented daughter. She would also have to abandon her art course and become a single mother, providing a home for her unborn child.

It was because of this chapter in what should have been the carefree days of her youth that Eleanor realised how easy it was to throw one's potential away and why she was so passionate about encouraging young people to believe in themselves and follow their dreams.

Her expectant child had been born three months premature and sadly did not survive. Strangely, Eleanor did not feel any relief as she thought she might, but instead went into deep depression at the thought of having lost a life, which she had partly created and which she would never know.

It was something which would never leave her and part of the reason why she knew she would never be able to have another child or form a relationship with someone who wanted children.

Since that chapter in her life, Eleanor had been wary of becoming involved in intimate relationships; there had been one or two male friends with whom she had become close but she was scared of the future. Since going into teaching, she found all her energy and time was taken up with the career to which she was committed. She knew her parents, now departed, would have dearly loved grandchildren or indeed to see their daughter settled in a loving relationship but they would never have dreamt of questioning Eleanor as to the reasons why this had never happened.

Her star pupils were Joel and Leila. Both had an obvious gift for art and art appreciation. She had studied their reactions on the school trip to the National Gallery and could see how looking at great art transported them to another world. Another world, far away, she suspected, from the reality of their own lives.

If only more young people from what was generally referred to as "disadvantaged backgrounds" were given the opportunity to experience great art, music and literature. Eleanor was convinced it would take them away from their lives of crime, drugs, petty thefts and, sadly, all too often, premature death.

She realised she could only play a very small part in this but she dreamt of a day when every child would have the opportunity to explore a world far removed from social media, pornographic films, trashy television programmes and all the other detritus which seemed to permeate the very soul of life in the twenty-first century.

"Good afternoon, everyone," Eleanor greeted Year 10 as they entered the art studio. Dressed in colourful materials, a flowing skirt, chiffon scarf and many silver bangles which jangled every time she moved her hands, Eleanor could have been the subject of a painting herself. "Today, I am going to suggest a theme which you may interpret however you wish."

She perched upon the end of a wooden table, which contained a still life composition, a vase of tulips and bowl of fruit, from the previous class.

This idea appealed to Joel and Leila who enthusiastically took their places ready to begin. One or two looked rather nervous at this proposal, whilst those who regarded art classes as an excuse for doing nothing mumbled amongst themselves.

Eleanor waited until they were all settled and had stopped chattering before announcing, "The theme is... my dream for the future."

They sat at the tables arranged around the large, white painted room whose walls were covered in various pictures produced by students of all ages and capabilities.

"You may paint in watercolours or oils, charcoal, pastels, acrylic, whatever you feel suits your subject."

The disinterested group huddled together in a corner, whispering about what they could do. Most of their ideas centred around sex, fast cars, fashion and portraying themselves as millionaires, living in massive mansions with swimming pools, their own cinemas, games rooms, gyms and an army of servants waiting upon them. "Living the dream" they called it.

Eleanor was pleased if they were inspired to paint anything, whatever the subject.

Leila sat at a table next to Joel. She was already creating images in her mind. At first, she had thought of her native landscape: the dramatic mountains, the desert lands, the beautiful blue sea and sky, and white sands, where her father and mother had once taken her and her siblings for a break away from the city. She did also love the bustle of the city, the busy narrow streets, the bazaars, the constant chattering of voices and chords of different ancient instruments echoing through the streets, the magnificent ancient buildings which had stood proudly for thousands of years, but upon reflection she knew that could only ever be a dream as so much of that beauty had been reduced to rubble and would take many years to restore to anything which resembled the original beauty.

Instead, Leila imagined a future for her mother and her siblings in England. A good job for herself, so that she could earn enough money to enable her mother to stop cleaning lavatories and bedrooms in cheap boarding houses. She would paint a picture of a home of their own with a garden, where they could plant a variety of beautiful flowers depicting all the shades of the rainbow, growing beside patches of scented herbs, which she and her mother would gather to flavour their favourite dishes. During summer days they would sit outdoors, listening to the sweet sound of the birdsong.

She would interpret this with bright colours in oils. A golden sunset, which reminded her of home. It was the same sun and the same moon which appeared in both countries, a common bond which, no matter where on Earth one was, it was possible to share the same experience of gazing at these heavenly bodies. Different shades of green, sage, emerald and jade, would represent the trees, shrubs and grass, whilst crimsons, purples, pinks, blues and other dramatic shades would represent exotic plants. She would paint a dream-like landscape.

Joel, in contrast, had chosen watercolours. He loved their softness and subtlety and the ability to portray an ethereal quality in their interpretation. He felt there was a spiritual dimension in a watercolour painting which was in contrast to the noise, inner turmoil and stress, which he felt in his own life and which he visualised in dramatic and bold colours: bright reds, deep purples, luminous oranges, greens and blues.

Quite what he would paint, he wasn't yet sure. He knew he wanted a work to reflect peace not just for himself and his mother but for the entire world. An illusory paradise perhaps!

Joel was aware that many authors had this vision: Thomas More's *Utopia*, Plato's *Symposium*, and he was aware of the debate as to which was the most important: art or literature.

Hesitantly, Joel took his first brush stroke and the canvas was covered in a pale blue which could represent sky or sea.

He wasn't yet sure. Perhaps a sea and upon it, a sailing ship on a journey to a paradise island, where the inhabitants who lived there were of every shape, sex and colour and despite speaking different languages lived in harmony, singing and dancing and feasting and loving.

He wasn't exactly sure how this represented a dream for his future as he couldn't imagine himself sailing across the seas to anywhere but he did nurture a hope that he might be able to play a small part in the creation of a better world. He would never have spoken of this to anyone, not even Leila, but subconsciously he had described his dream through painting.

Eleanor looked at her watch. She hated time limits when her pupils were being creative. "Class, we have half an hour left, but please take your time as you can finish your paintings next week."

"We've finished, miss," the group in the corner at the back of the classroom chanted.

Eleanor had ignored their guffaws and snorts throughout the lesson. She walked across the room towards the group and leant over them to inspect their work.

She wasn't surprised to see images of phalluses and vaginas. In fact, she explained, much to their amusement, that the art world had always interpreted the human anatomy in various forms from the earliest civilisations. Some of these images were surprisingly well drawn. However, Eleanor did find the interpretation disturbing. The spent spliffs, guns and knives were painted in layers of thick, black oils, surrounded by heavy daubs of deep, red paint representing the blood splattered all around them. Sadly, this was the lives they knew and to which they aspired.

Eleanor was aware of the smirks upon their faces, hoping to shock her with their graffiti art.

Instead, she smiled slowly. "Some of these are very good," she pronounced, shocking them into silence, "As contemporary works of art."

She picked up one canvas and held it in front of the class. There was some muffled laughter and a few were genuinely shocked. Joel and Leila exchanged glances.

"Has anyone any comment to make?" Eleanor wanted to start a discussion.

Joel raised his hand. "I think it's good and I get the gun and knife stuff but isn't that the lives they lead now? I thought we were supposed to paint a dream for our futures and surely they would prefer a future without weapons of fear and evil."

"And how do you suggest we get that, wise boy?" It was Jamal who spoke. "It's all we know, innit, and how are we ever gonna change that? Thems our protection against an evil society!"

Joel knew Jamal had been recruited into Jordan's gang as a runner too.

A heavy silence descended, as if a giant cloud had enveloped the room.

In that single moment, Eleanor realised she had misjudged her "naughty group". Whereas she had immediately discovered the talents of her star pupils Joel and Leila, she had all too quickly dismissed those who showed no interest in her lessons, without challenging their reasons for their supposed boredom. She felt guilty for not giving them more understanding and encouragement. She doubted they had ever been praised in their young lives or encouraged to pursue their dreams.

"That's a good point you raise," Eleanor said with sincerity and turning to Joel. "Joel, would you like to reply to Jamal?"

Joel was unprepared for Eleanor's suggestion. He knew where Jamal and his mates were coming from and understood why they all carried knives for self-protection and who was he to criticise? He carried a knife too but no one suspected him of doing such a thing, with his almost pretty baby face, well-groomed hair and clean school uniform. Adults automatically assumed that youngsters, like Jamal, whose fathers were often absent and whose mothers had several children by different men and who sometimes were forced to sell their bodies in order to make enough money to pay the rent and buy food, were doomed to a life of crime. But Joel himself knew how easy it was to get dragged into the drugs and street gang scene.

"Yes, I understand where Jamal is coming from. He doesn't have a choice when everyone carries weapons 'cause they never know when they might need to protect themselves."

Eleanor wondered whether Joel carried a knife. She could see Leila was dying to add her voice to the discussion.

"Leila, do you want to say something?"

Leila had a soft voice and was usually too shy to speak in class but she was obviously moved to do so.

"I just wanted to say that it doesn't matter how bad you might think things are, there's always a way out. When my house was bombed and my brothers, sisters and grandparents were killed and aunts, uncles and cousins were tortured, my mother, who had already lost her husband, could so easily have given up on life. What was there to live for? But we kept going. We had each other and my sister and brother, who had survived, needed us. Also, my mother was pregnant with my younger brother and so we needed to stay positive and think towards the future. We made ourselves believe in a better life, no matter how difficult that journey might be and despite the fact that my younger brother did not make it."

She fell silent, lost in thoughts and memories of the ordeals they had faced.

She had never mentioned a younger brother not making the journey before.

Eleanor was moved by Leila's words and from the silence which fell upon the class, she hoped that many of the others might be too.

"Thank you, Leila," she said. "I think we can all learn a lesson from your wise words."

The atmosphere was broken by the shrill sound of the bell heralding the end of the lesson. It had come too soon for Eleanor and the students who were all engrossed in the topic of conversation.

"Heavens, that time already," Eleanor said. "If you wish to continue this discussion next week, we can."

Several heads nodded.

"Jamal, Marick, Wayne, if I may, I would like to display your work upon the studio walls. Perhaps not the breasts and penises." She smiled. "Although they are very well drawn."

"Thems what we wants for our future, miss," Wayne said with a cheeky grin.

Leila blushed and Joel was embarrassed for her.

"Yes, I think I understood that, Wayne, thank you," Eleanor said calmly. "But the subject is rather too adult for some of the younger pupils who'll be using the art room. However, I think the weapons are competently drawn and should be displayed and hopefully will make everyone think about their meaning and the consequences. Right, now off you go and thank you for an interesting session."

"Might I also suggest," Eleanor raised her voice as the class began to file out of the classroom, "That between now and the next lesson you contemplate futures to which you might aspire! Don't accept that you are doomed to remain in your present situations; imagine what you could achieve if you set your mind to it."

There was a certain amount of muttering and grumbling as they left the art studio but Eleanor knew that one or two of them would mull over what she had said.

Joel left school that day feeling inspired and optimistic. At home, his mother was much happier now she had Tony for a companion. He hadn't noticed the usual highs and lows of her moods, which had been a result of her dependence upon drugs. He was sure this was due to the influence of Tony, who had been through that journey in the seventies. Joel dared to wonder whether there was any need for him to work anymore for Jordan and his gang, but he knew that trying to get out of it wouldn't be easy.

One first year boy, who lived with a violent father and a mother with mental health issues, had been seduced into joining a gang as he felt it offered friendship and even love, which was something he never experienced at home. He believed the leader really cared about him and agreed to take the train to Northampton, where he would be met by strangers and driven to some seedy rooms, somewhere the drugs would be swapped for the money. This particular boy was set upon by the main dealer, who threatened him with a knife unless he allowed him to abuse him and as he attempted to protest, and in desperation, the boy bit the dealer's arm. As a result, his assailant knifed him through the heart. When the headmaster announced the sad news that the boy had been fatally wounded, no one knew or asked for any details and assumed it was his father who had killed him.

When Joel was told the gory details by Jordan, he felt sad for the boy and nervous for himself.

Leila walked part of the way home with him. This had become a regular pattern if they both finished school at the same time.

"It's so sad those boys today, don't you think?" she said, her tiny steps struggling to keep up with his strong stride. "And to think they carry knives with them. That is so dangerous."

Joel lowered his head and looked at the grass beneath their feet. He hoped she did not suspect him of anything. She was very perceptive. He would hate for her to know that he carried a knife inside his sweatshirt or that he was a runner for drug dealers. She would probably never speak to him again.

"It's the only way they know," he said.

"But their mothers and fathers. Do they know?"

"Not all parents are as loving and caring as yours were, Leila, and like your mum is now. Lots of kids have parents who are drug addicts themselves and don't care what their sons or daughters do."

"That's really sad," Leila said quietly.

They had arrived at the ancient oak tree which was the place where they parted and went their separate ways across the common.

"See you tomorrow." Leila turned away from him, the colourful chiffon scarf which covered her head flowing behind her. She did not have to cover her head as her religion did not dictate the covering of heads but she liked to wear chiffon or silk scarves depicting designs which, for Leila, represented a kaleidoscope of the imagination.

"Sure." Joel began walking in the opposite direction, deep in thought.

He had just arrived home when his mobile vibrated in his pocket. He took it out and immediately recognised the number.

Jordan's voice bellowed. "Get your effing arse down 'ere right away. I've got a big job."

Joel was about to protest as he had a lot of homework and really did not want to go to meet drug dealers, but he knew he had no choice as Jordan and his gang mates would only start threatening him.

"Hello, darling." Gemma heard the front door close. "Good day?"

Joel kissed his mother on the cheek. "Yeah, not bad, but I've just remembered I've got to go back to school. It's an art project we're doing and I've left all my stuff there and need to print some papers out."

"Oh, that's a shame. Tony wanted to take us out to see the new James Bond movie. It's on in the West End. How long will you be?"

"Sorry, Mum. Sounds great but you go without me. I'll see it some other time."

"Oh, he will be disappointed. Will you get yourself some supper then?"

"Don't worry, I'll be fine." Joel turned to go. "See yer."

"Took yer time. You're late." Jordan was stamping up and down behind their appointed meeting place on the other side of the common. The run-down bus shelter with shattered glass and badly in need of a coat of paint was an eyesore.

He was sporting the latest pair of Alexander McQueen trainers and no doubt expecting Joel to admire them.

"I came as soon as I got your message."

"S'pose you were trying to shag that Arabic bitch."

"She's Yazidi and she's not a bitch," Joel said protectively. "Anyway, I was at home and was going to the cinema with my mum."

"Tough shit." Jordan lit a spliff. "Here." He thrust a package into Joel's hand and muttered an address, telling him to forget it as soon as he'd delivered it. If he didn't do as he was told, his life would be in danger.

Joel's heart sank. He really did not want to do this anymore but like an animal caught in a trap, there seemed to be no escape route.

"You need to take a train," Jordan said.

"Where to?" Joel was alarmed.

"St. Pancras to Bedford," he said in a matter-of-fact manner.

"Where's that?"

"About forty-five minutes away. Don't look so shit scared. You're a big boy!"

"But my mum will be worried if I'm late back."

"That's your problem."

"What about a train ticket?" Joel had no money on him.

Jordon laughed. "You could make a mint on this job, so don't f—k it up."

Jordan stood over him, shoulders hunched, hands in pockets and a hoody pulled well over his face. He was pacing from side to side on his feet and glancing nervously around him as if in preparation for a quick getaway.

"Don't expect me to give you money for a train ticket!"

"I don't have any ready cash on me," Joel said.

Reluctantly, Jordan put his hand in the pocket of his tracksuit and produced a wad of notes. He pushed a twenty pound note in Joel's hand. "I want this back, right?"

Joel nodded, eager to get away.

"Beat it," Jordan commanded. "And make sure you keep out of the way of any police."

Joel turned and headed off, checking his knife was safely tucked beneath his sweatshirt.

He would get the tube to St. Pancras. He really didn't know North London well. He would have to call his mother and make some excuse for being late home. Then he remembered she and Tony were going to the cinema in Leicester Square so hopefully he might be back before them if he could get a fast train to Bedford and back.

The train took forty-five minutes and was packed with commuters travelling home from their offices in London. Joel studied their demeanours. Some had their heads lowered looking at their mobiles, one or two were actually reading paperbacks. Joel was fascinated to know their taste in literature and craned his neck to read some of the titles. A young woman took a copy of *The Girl on the Train* from her designer bag, a middle-aged male, seatless and standing beside the toilet door, was absorbed in *The Whistler* by John Grisham. Joel didn't have a clue what stories unfolded between the pages of these novels but was fascinated at how absorbed these passengers seemed amidst the general jostling and noise of the commuter carriage.

Studying their tired expressions, he pondered whether they were really happy with their existence, following the same pattern day in, day out. He assumed they were earning good money and, of course, that was a valid reason for the constant travelling to and from work. However, for Joel there was something of a mechanised army about the process.

Joel stepped off at Bedford Station, which he thought unremarkable. He had vaguely hoped that, being out of London, it might be rather old and quaint like the photographs of old England in an edition of a history book, which his father had won at school. It was the one object which his mother had not removed and still stood stiffly as a guard at Buckingham Palace, propped between the hardback travel, art and music books, which lined the shelves above his mother's volumes of fiction, mainly paperbacks. He remembered his father hammering the shelves into the cheap wall and cursing when he banged his thumb, instead of a nail, with the hammer. Both his parents had enjoyed reading but his mother rarely picked up a book anymore. Joel loved browsing between the pages of the large illustrated editions and in particular the glossy art books. Now that he had decided he would like to be an artist, he would often refer to them after a lesson.

Instead, like so many county towns, the original station had succumbed to being replaced by a modern, unprepossessing building retaining none of the character of the original Victorian station. The slate-coloured sky added to the depressing atmosphere and the charcoal clouds threatened an imminent storm.

He had only just stepped outside the station when a tall Asian boy with a hood pulled well over his face came towards him.

"Yo, come 'ere," he commanded. "Gimme that."

He took the bag from Joel and Joel sighed with relief thinking he could turn around and take the next train back to London.

Before he could make his escape, however, another man appeared and, muttering something incomprehensible to the young boy, they ushered a petrified Joel into a beaten-up old van parked in the station car park. Inside the vehicle was a third person sitting in the driving seat. The older man barked a command and instantly the driver started the engine and sped off down the nearby road.

Out of the back seat of the car where he sat huddled between the two men who had met him, Joel glanced at tall, grey Victorian houses, whose paint peeling doors and shabby window curtains had obviously seen better days. Once, the town had been the destination of professional people, many moving there in order to educate their offspring at the elite public schools.

After speeding around various back streets, the van stopped in front of a narrow, shabby house with filthy windows where torn sheets were used as curtains. A few teenagers loitered menacingly at the bottom of the steps leading up to the front door. Joel's companions ordered him to follow them into the house. A sheet of cardboard was placed in the top half of the door, where once there would have been a pane of multi-coloured stained glass. The younger boy pressed the door bell and an ashen faced figure peered out of an open window on the first floor.

"That 'im?" he shouted to the men now clinging onto Joel. "Hardly looks out of nappies."

"Inside," the first dealer shouted and shoved Joel in front of him.

The narrow hallway was dark and depressing and the carpet was threadbare and stained, emitting an odious smell reminiscent of the stairwell leading to Joel's flat. Joel climbed the stairs in front of the men, who then pushed him forcefully into a first-floor room and told to wait. The others disappeared into a different room and he heard a door slam shut. He looked around him. Scary African masks hung on the walls and a pair of shabby sofas were positioned in the middle of the room. The floorboards were bare, apart from a brightly coloured ethnic rug which lifted the gloomy atmosphere.

Joel was thirsty and hungry. He also needed a pee but was far too scared to attempt to find a loo.

After what seemed like hours, the dealers returned and pushed the canvas bag back into Joel's hands. He noticed the enormous gold rings on their fingers and chains around their necks. If they were making so much money out of drugs, Joel wondered why they didn't live in palaces but he supposed places like this were just a front.

He found himself being shunted outside again, blinking in the daylight after the darkness of the interior and thrust into the van, where the driver sat waiting. Driving back to the station, one of the men took out a knife and pretended to put it against Joel's throat.

"You make sure you deliver that bag unopened or you'll end up five foot under." His breath smelt foul, a mixture of ganja and bad breath.

Joel couldn't stop himself from shaking and was afraid he might wet himself as well.

"I think you're a pussy foot." He held the knife close to Joel again, laughing and showing one gold and one missing tooth.

The van screeched into the car park and Joel found himself practically being thrown out onto the ground. Clutching the bag, Joel stumbled up the steps and into the station. He was now bursting for the loo but saw a train about to leave and jumped on it, finding a seat to himself and breathing a huge sigh of relief. He had never been so frightened in his life.

As the train pulled out of the station, a clap of thunder echoed around the sky as the heavens opened and rain in the form of hailstones pummelled against the carriage windows.

It seemed an appropriate end to a deeply depressing and menacing evening.

That night, Joel could not sleep. He had put both the knife and the bag containing the money under his pillow. He knew he would have to be at school really early as Jordan would be waiting to take the money.

Fortunately, his mother and Tony did not return home until the early hours of the morning, so had no idea of how he had spent his evening. He'd heard his mother giggling a lot and was pleased she sounded so happy. Tony was always the perfect gentleman and always saw Gemma home but never stayed the night. He had on occasions mentioned the idea of Joel and Gemma moving into his Georgian house in Chelsea. He had explained that there was a maisonette on the top floor where they could be quite self-sufficient. Gemma had said that it was kind of him and she would think about it. Joel hoped she would agree and he could go to a new school and hopefully get away from Jordan and the whole wretched drug business.

He wished he could take Leila with him but he would certainly make sure that she came to visit them and hopefully stay sometimes. They could explore Chelsea together. Joel had always been fascinated by houses with blue plaques on their walls, saying which famous person once lived there. He remembered his father taking him once to Brook Street in Mayfair and showing him a plaque on a house where Jimi Hendrix once lived. Joel had never heard of Jimi Hendrix but his father told him that he was the greatest guitarist who ever lived.

"Will you take me to see him, Dad?" a young Joel asked enthusiastically.

His father took his hand in his and, with his black eyes fixed upon his young son, said quietly, "Sadly, son, he is no longer with us."

"Oh." Joel supposed it meant that Jimi was actually dead and had not simply moved to another place or country. "What happened to him?"

"Well, despite being so talented at playing the guitar…" His father paused. "He got into bad habits and started to take things which made him sick."

"You mean, he ate too many sweets?" A bright-eyed Joel looked adoringly up at his handsome father.

Lloyd smiled gently. He knew the reason for Joel suggesting sweets was because Gemma was always telling him that if he ate too many sweets, he would make himself sick.

"Well, not sweets, Joel, no. But it was a substance which made him feel good at first and then he couldn't stop. Just remember, if you ever find yourself tempted by bad people to do bad things, always walk away or it can destroy your whole life."

Although very young, Joel had never forgotten his father's words that day as they stood outside the Jimi Hendrix house and when he was old enough to realise it was drugs which had destroyed the guitarist, he thought how silly he had been and what a shame it was that he died so young. Not long after Joel had those thoughts, his father took him aside to explain that he had betrayed Joel and Gemma and was going away to prison as a punishment.

CHAPTER SIX

The following day, Joel couldn't wait to see Leila. She had brought some stability into his life in her calm and quiet way. However, she wasn't at school. He texted her and she replied that they had received bad news from Yemen and she could not leave her mother alone.

Will you be in tomorrow? he texted.

I hope so, came the reply.

Then tell me all about it.

There was no reply.

Jordan, as usual, had been waiting to take the payment from Joel. He told him he'd have to wait for his own share as someone in the county lines gang had done a runner, taking thousands of pounds, so the big boss was a bit short of ready cash at the moment.

The following day, Leila did come into school but seemed very preoccupied and Joel did not want to bombard her with questions. Instead, he hoped she would confide in him as they walked home.

"My mother had relations who had reached Syria and who were hoping eventually to join us here. They had been travelling from Yemen ever since our city was bombed and wherever they tried to settle, the bombing and destruction followed them. They were caught in the fighting between the rebels and Syrian government in Aleppo.

"My uncle, who was my mother's brother, was a hospital doctor, like my father, and refused to stop working despite the constant threat of airstrikes. He was working as a surgeon in the local hospital, trying to save the lives of so many innocent victims. Many of whom were children. He and his family thought they had found a safe place for a while and hoped life would return to some normality as the shops began to open and people dared to walk in the streets again but then the indiscriminate bombing began again.

"He left my aunt and their five children in the block of flats, where they were renting a small apartment, to go to the hospital. When he returned in the evening, instead of the flats, there was nothing but rubble and mutilated bodies lying in rivers of blood amidst the stench of death. He has lost his entire family." She could not control the tears. "And now we'll never see them again. He is my mother's only surviving relation. She had lost everyone else and she prayed every night for him and his family to arrive safely in England."

Joel took a deep breath. What she had described seemed a whole world away, as indeed it was, and he doubted he would have been aware of such suffering if he had not met Leila.

"I'm so sorry." He could hardly imagine such horrors, the destruction, the cruelty, the loss of lives and all for what, he asked himself. Certainly not freedom or a better life.

The people had lost homes, jobs, families and friends. They had travelled hundreds of miles on foot with only the clothes they stood up in. They had no choice but to live in refugee camps, where health and hygiene were a constant threat. Many were tortured if captured. The children sat around in the dirt, hollow eyed and hungry, unable to comprehend the reality of what was happening to them.

"I must hurry." Leila turned to face Joel.

With the late afternoon sunlight catching the outline of her slim figure, Joel thought how beautiful and yet how fragile she looked. He would have loved to put his arms around her and tell her he would always be there for her but, of course, he knew such a gesture was not appropriate.

"My mother will be waiting and I should be there to help her to look after my sister and brother."

"Of course." Joel nodded. "And if there's anything I can do, please give me a call."

"Thank you." She adjusted the long scarf draped around her head. In contrast to her usual brightly coloured scarf, today it was dark grey in mourning for her lost loved ones.

In the art lesson that week, Eleanor announced she had a surprise for the class. She explained that she had a friend who was the guardian of a beautiful country house and whose owner possessed one of the best private collections of paintings in England. Eleanor had arranged for a coach to take them all to visit the house during the last week of term.

To her surprise, everyone appeared enthusiastic. There were no groans or swear words from Jamal and his mates, who normally would not have considered such an outing "cool" and, of course, the more competent students, and especially Joel and Leila, were thrilled. It was a day to look forward to.

However, Leila did confide in Joel that she would not feel happy leaving her mother and siblings but he pointed out it was some time away and it would only be like going to school all day anyway.

CHAPTER SEVEN

The Honourable Mark Botellier-Humphries was the eleventh generation of his family to inherit Botellier Hall, a sprawling country mansion which had various wings added over the centuries. The first Baron Botellier descended from William the Conqueror and had been given acres of land, upon which he could graze sheep and build a house, as a thank you for helping to lead his troops to victory at the Battle of Hastings.

Another descendent had been handsomely rewarded by Queen Elizabeth I for commanding a galleon in the Spanish Armada. The generosity of the queen guaranteed the living and education for the next five generations of Botelliers who considered themselves true aristocrats with more blue blood than the royal family.

Mark, now in his forty-ninth year, had been divorced twice, sired five children from whom he was estranged and was now living with a well-known model, half his age. He also had a suspended prison sentence for driving his Aston Martin under the influence of alcohol and drugs.

The estate, which had once provided work and homes for most of the local village, was now mostly neglected and the repairs needed on the hall were taking Mark more and more into the abyss of debt, whilst he continued to squander his inheritance on drink, drugs and gambling.

Once, there had been a stable of fine horses, bred for racing, but these too had been sold to pay off debts. His children's education was paid for by a family trust but his ex-wives did not receive a penny from him.

The only people employed at the hall were Mrs Moreton, a matronly villager who came part time to cook his meals, her young daughter who cleaned to earn money to save towards her expenses when she went to train as a nurse the following year, a part-time gardener, and Timothy Stratton whom Eleanor had known since art school. She loved Tim, not in a sexual way as she always knew his preferences lay with the male sex, but he was the kindest person she had ever met.

Unable to make a living as an artist, he had taught in a London comprehensive for many years until he had met an ex-Etonian on Hampstead Heath who introduced him to a whole new set of society people. Suddenly, Tim found himself dining in expensive, fashionable restaurants, holidaying in the Mediterranean on board the luxury yachts of self-made billionaires and rock stars. It was a lifestyle Tim never dreamt of when he was growing up in a small Welsh village where his father farmed and his mother ran a second-hand bookshop.

Tim had never lost his principles and insisted on continuing to teach, hoping to inspire the most disadvantaged pupils he encountered in the classroom. There was nothing to match the pleasure he gained when just one young boy or girl began to appreciate the treasures of the art world and the talent and dedication of the artists who pursued their vision throughout their lives, often for little reward. Tim wished that schools concentrated more upon art and music, which he believed had the capacity to enrich even the most philistine heart.

Drugs were always freely available in Tim's new world but his addiction was alcohol and had he not been told by a Harley Street consultant, paid for by his boyfriend, that unless he gave up alcohol his liver would fail and that within twelve months he would be dead, then he probably would not have been alive today.

"We're going to a country house weekend, darling," Jeffrey, who, having been the beneficiary of a trust set up by his parents, didn't need to work for a living but earned a fortune by being an interior designer to the rich and famous, had announced one Friday morning. "So, chop, chop. Sanders is picking us up at midday."

Sanders was Jeffrey's personal driver who was always on call.

They were sitting at the breakfast table in their bijou Chelsea house and Jeffrey was dipping his last toasted soldier into his lightly boiled egg. Tim was always amused by this habit which he had carried into adulthood from the nursery, when his nanny used to cut his toast into soldiers every teatime and which he would duly dip into the bright yellow yoke oozing from the delicate shell.

Jeffrey always took breakfast in his elegant, pure silk, Japanese kimono, displaying a design of exotic pink flamingos.

"But I have a lesson today, Jeffrey," Tim protested. "I can't let them down." He reached for the marmalade and began spreading it on his toast in a slightly agitated manner.

"Oh, don't be so pathetic," Jeffrey retorted. "I've told you before to give up that poxy teaching job of yours. Those comprehensive kids will never learn to appreciate art. They'd rather be out stabbing each other. Far more fun."

"That's not fair. There's as much talent in that school as there ever was in your posh public boarding establishment. They just don't always get the chance to have it discovered, that's all." Tim crunched the toast between his teeth.

Jeffrey stood up to refill the teapot and returning to the table, after placing the pot down, gave Tim a hug from behind.

"How sweet. So, Saint Timothy is going to save the working classes and convert them to high culture?"

"Don't be such a snob." Tim turned round to face Jeffrey, his face turning puce. "A lot of talent has come from working-class backgrounds: musicians, artists, writers, political leaders."

"God, don't go down the political path. When good old aristocrats like Churchill and Macmillan were in charge, you knew where you were but with your Harold Wilsons and Tony Blairs, the whole bloody art of leadership and governing fell apart. Name me one member of parliament who is capable of giving a Churchillian speech today."

Tim ignored this last remark.

"Anyway, just because it's a comprehensive doesn't mean it's all one class, although I hate that word anyway. There are pupils from all backgrounds and nationalities and believe me, they go out into the world a lot better educated for living and mixing with all types of people than your narrow-minded public school types."

Jeffrey returned to his seat and poured himself another cup of tea. Tim preferred coffee first thing in the morning.

Jeffrey hated arguments, especially with Tim whom he adored. Arguments reminded him of his unhappy childhood when, lying in bed, he would frequently press his chubby hands hard against his ears, attempting to shut out the raised voices of his parents as they verbally fought with each other downstairs.

Jeffrey's parents had always been aloof. His father was an army man and they had travelled a great deal around the world. Jeffrey was an only child and sent off to boarding school at seven years of age when his parents were posted to the Middle East. His guardian was his mother's unmarried sister who lived in Windsor.

He would write to his mother from school, begging them to let him travel with them but to no avail. He wasn't particularly missing his mother and father, but he loathed being at boarding school and longed for adventure.

Jeffrey didn't know it, but even had his mother wanted to have her son home, she was having far too much fun as an army wife, not to mention the numerous affairs which she conducted around the globe.

When Jeffrey left school and announced he was not going to university and that he was "gay", his father refused to have anything to do with him until he came to his senses.

Two months later, on his nineteenth birthday, Jeffrey's mother was killed in a car crash and he inherited a considerable amount of money. His father had remarried by the end of the year and Jeffrey never saw him again. He was, however, left a second legacy in a trust fund when his father died. His home and possessions went to his second wife, but he had obviously forgotten the trust fund he'd set up for Jeffrey when he was born.

Jeffrey had invested his mother's money in starting up an interior design business and it had flourished. It was a time when everyone who could afford it wanted a professional to decorate and furnish their home. Jeffrey had no training, but assumed he had merely inherited good taste, plus, of course, possessing a certain flair for design. He was always immaculately dressed and had a way of charming his prospective clients, especially when he embellished his connections with certain members of the royal family.

Tim was the first person to have shown Jeffrey real affection and later true love.

"What time are you able to get away then?" Jeffrey asked more gently.

Tim looked at his watch. "Well, not until 3:30."

"Right, I'll get Sanders to collect me from here at 3 p.m. and we'll come to the school for you at 3:30, so make sure you have everything you need packed before you go off this morning and I can bring it with me. Oh, and you'd better throw in a dinner jacket and bow tie, just in case."

Tim finished his toast and coffee and stood up. "Fine. I'll get packed now."

He made his way towards the stairs. He would have much preferred to spend their weekend together at the opera or ballet or a movie, but he knew Jeffrey enjoyed social gatherings and meeting people and, to be fair, it didn't happen every weekend.

Jeffrey and Tim arrived at Botellier Hall at 6 o'clock, the perfect time, as Jeffrey pronounced, for an "apero". Mark Botellier-Humphries, an old school friend of Jeffrey's, greeted the pair warmly as they were shown into one of the elegant drawing rooms. Jeffrey had offered to give his services as an interior designer for free, knowing that with Mark's inner circle of friends, who would have the opportunity to admire the newly decorated rooms, he would gain commissions, which he did.

Tim often pondered how strange it was that a talented and successful rock star or fashionable model or CEO of a company felt the need to have a stranger design their surroundings. One would expect them to want to demonstrate their own taste as an extension of their personality and ego. He suspected it was more to do with their wish to imitate the upper classes!

With their acquired wealth, the newly rich and famous could now educate their children at the best schools and buy grand townhouses and country estates, but not having aristocratic backgrounds themselves and being feted by the very people they wished to imitate, they needed to make sure they could meet and entertain their new acquaintances on an equal footing. Hence Jeffrey had a marvellous time choosing the right art and furnishings and attending the most prestigious auctions spending other people's money.

"Welcome, dear boy." Mark lunged at Tim and proffered a kiss upon his cheek which barely brushed past his lips.

Jeffrey looked on. He was not surprised Mark was attracted to Tim who had the fine features of a Greek god as represented in ancient sculptures. His classical features were perfectly proportioned and flaxen curls framed his pale face. Mark himself was a large man with a boyish cherubic face. He was flamboyantly dressed in a maroon velvet suit and patterned brocade waistcoat.

It was common knowledge in Mark's intimate circles that he was equally attracted to males and females.

Tim was somewhat embarrassed but immediately drawn towards Mark, a larger-than-life character, who obviously gained immense pleasure from making other people happy and sharing his beautiful home and works of art.

"You're the first to arrive, but I'm so glad you made it. It's going to be a fun weekend. There are some very interesting people coming."

"Looking forward to it." Jeffrey smiled enthusiastically.

On weekends when Mark entertained, he would ask the housekeeper to bring her daughter to help with the guests' rooms and whatever else was needed. He insisted preparations were of the highest standard.

As a young man, his father had taken him to Sandringham in Norfolk, where they had stayed as guests of the queen. No sooner had they arrived than their overnight suitcases were whisked away upstairs. Upon entering their bedrooms, the contents of the overnight suitcases had been removed, dinner suits hung in vast wardrobes, pyjamas neatly folded and placed upon the bed, and shirts beautifully pressed so that not a hint of a crease appeared and hung beside the suits. All underwear had similarly been pressed and allocated drawers.

Mark had never forgotten this visit and vowed that his own house guests would be treated exactly the same as those of royalty.

"So, gentlemen, what takes your fancy?" Mark gestured towards a mahogany Georgian sideboard where every type of alcoholic drink appeared to be lined up.

Tim was hesitant.

"Try the Singapore slings, they're lethal." Jeffrey nudged Tim and winked at Mark.

"Maybe not, in that case," Tim said. "I want to enjoy the evening and we've only just arrived."

"Quite right," Mark agreed, pouring himself another large whisky. "May I suggest a glass of Dom P?"

Tim looked slightly puzzled.

"Dom Perignon..." Mark picked up a bottle. "Champers."

"Sounds perfect." Tim allowed Mark to pour him a glass and Jeffrey decided to follow suit.

"I do have a young chap from the village who is supposed to be serving drinks, but he's a tad late."

At that point, a lean, long-haired teenager rushed into the drawing room. "I'm sorry, sir, my scooter broke down at the bottom of your drive, so I 'ad to leave it there and walk the rest of the way."

Jeffrey could sympathise as the drive to the hall must be at least two miles long.

Jamie, the young man, was wearing jeans and a white T-shirt with the slogan of a heavy metal band written across the chest. Mark would have preferred him to wear something more professional but decided against making any comment. He was fortunate to have Jamie helping him at all.

The loud roar of a Ferrari was heard outside in the drive, shattering the peaceful atmosphere which had prevailed in the hall. The housekeeper opened the front door and showed a tall, young man with unusual but interesting features into the room. His shiny, dark hair was almost shoulder length and a floppy fringe hung over his forehead. He was wearing a black silk shirt and purple velvet cords and an equally tall, blonde-haired young woman with stunning model looks accompanied him.

Tim and Jeffrey immediately recognised the pair.

Peter Darcy was the lead singer of the most popular band in the UK and Claudia Tompkins was a top model and one of Peter's many girlfriends.

"Darcy, come and meet my dear friends: Jeffrey Hamilton-Moore, the most sought-after interior designer in London, and his partner Tim. I'm sorry, Tim, I didn't catch what you do."

Tim looked somewhat embarrassed. "I teach art," he said sipping his champagne.

"And a brilliant artist in his own right," Jeffrey added, patting Tim proudly on the shoulder.

"Oh, if you're interested in art, you must see my collection. Handed down through generations and second only to Her Majesty's, I believe."

Peter and Claudia were being proffered glasses of champagne by Jamie, who had become quite overcome by being so close to his favourite singer in the flesh.

"Oh yeah," Peter addressed Tim, "Mark's collection is really cool. In fact, I never tire of looking at it every time I come here. I'm still trying to persuade him to let me buy one of his Picassos."

"Ah, dear boy, if you persist long enough, you never know, you may succeed. Money simply doesn't last so long these days." Mark lifted his glass.

Tim glanced around at his surroundings. The grand pieces of antique furniture, the priceless Ming dynasty vases, the Persian carpeted floor, the heavy, velvet drapes hanging at the long, elegant windows which looked out onto the beautiful landscaped gardens. Tim wondered why Mark, when surrounded by such beauty, felt the need to take drugs, which would no doubt cause him to suffer a premature death in addition to diminishing his once vast wealth.

Other guests were now arriving. Tim recognised many of the faces: a politician, a writer, a photographer, a few actors, a classical musician. All were familiar faces in the fashionable publications of the day. And in the media.

Mark was winding his way, with glass in hand, between the company and attempting to introduce individuals to those with whom he thought there might be a mutual interest. He gained a great deal of pleasure from bringing people together. Nothing pleased him more than to hear someone say, "Well, of course, it was the Honourable Mark Botellier-Humphries who first introduced us."

Dinner was due to be served at 9 o'clock in the Napoleon dining room, where lithographs and original paintings of the Napoleonic Wars, which were a legacy from one of Mark's French ancestors whom had actually served with Napoleon and fought at the Battle of Waterloo, as did an uncle from the English side of Mark's family but alongside the Duke of Wellington.

Everyone started to make their way into the picture gallery where Jamie had his work cut out keeping glasses of champagne replenished. For Tim, this was the highlight of his evening and as he and Jeffrey entered the long, corridor-like room where every inch of wall space was covered in paintings, prints, lithographs and etchings, Tim was not disappointed.

They had both changed into dinner suits, as had most of the guests, apart from Peter, who remained in his black silk shirt and purple velvet cords, and a writer, who seemed to have a supercilious air about him and who sported a multi-coloured velvet jacket and matching bow tie. Claudia, looking stunning in a cream evening gown of satin brocade reminiscent of a period wedding gown, walked between the musician and the author, head bowed and giving the impression of hanging upon their every word as they conducted a conversation across her. Around her neck was a necklace of sparkling diamonds, a gift no doubt from Peter.

Suddenly, Tim was aware of the trio having stopped just behind him as he stood before a genuine Caravaggio.

"Mind blowing," Peter said. "He was the bad boy of his time," he explained to Claudia.

"Indeed," Tim agreed. "He was always getting involved in brawls, duels and even killed a man and was forced to flee Naples to Malta. He did everything he could to persuade the pope to pardon him and when he eventually did, it was too late. He died of a fever, aged thirty-seven. Yes, he was a genius with a paintbrush. Think of what he could have achieved had he lived into old age."

"Are you an artist?" Claudia seemed genuinely interested in Tim's commentary.

"Once I aspired to be," Tim said, "But sadly, I realised I didn't possess the ability to be a truly great one." He smiled at Claudia, realising just how beautiful she was and somehow there was an air of fragility about her, which reminded him of Botticelli's Venus.

"So, what do you do?" she persevered.

Peter was still engrossed in the painting.

"I teach," Tim said, somewhat flatly.

"Oh, really? Do you give private lessons? I would love to learn how to paint properly. I loved art at school, but it was not considered academic enough if one wanted to get into Oxbridge. Which I didn't. I knew I wasn't capable anyway, but they still insisted on Latin instead of art."

"Yes, I'm afraid art has been considered the least academic subject in schools for many years, but in reality, it encompasses a wealth of knowledge and is also accessible to everyone." Tim paused. "But in answer to your question, no, I don't give private tuition."

Claudia looked disappointed. "Well, if you ever change your mind, I would love to learn more."

Jeffrey had been accosted by a TV presenter of "reality shows", which, never having watched one, meant he had no idea who this large bosomed Amazon with the fake tan and copper-coloured hair was. However, he was left in no doubt when she introduced herself in a mid-Atlantic drawl.

"Hi, I'm Melissa Andrews. You may have seen my television shows."

"I'm afraid I don't watch a great deal of television," Jeffrey retorted.

"Ah well," she persevered. "My new series is getting people to change their décor and I hear you're the 'must have' interior designer to go to."

Jeffrey was wondering how he could extricate himself from this loud lioness with the low-cut dress, displaying heaving breasts every time she launched into conversation.

"I would love to have your advice on the series," she continued, sipping her champagne.

For a moment, Jeffrey was almost tempted to listen to her proposition, but then realised there was no way he would be able to work with this woman, despite the prospect of perhaps being on television, which appealed to his vanity.

Having caught up with Tim, Jeffrey was pleased to see the select group surrounding him and hanging on his every word. The beautiful girlfriend of Peter Darcy was obviously asking Tim whether he would give her art tuition.

"You could teach Claudia." Jeffrey never missed an opportunity and already his mind was musing upon the possibility of having Peter and Claudia as clients.

"Yeah." It was Peter who spoke, turning his attention away from the painting and facing Tim. "Why not? I think it's a great idea. Claude needs something to keep her occupied when I'm on tour."

Tim could believe that Peter would prefer Claudia was kept busy when he was away as he imagined she must have every eligible bachelor in London waiting to ask her out.

"Oh, please, will you think about it?" Claudia persisted.

Tim was flattered by her enthusiasm. "Very well. I'll give it some thought, although teaching keeps me pretty busy."

Claudia thanked him and moved on with Peter at her side. Tim supposed that people like Claudia and Peter were used to having their own way and he admitted the idea of giving lessons to the stunning model was tempting, though daunting.

Tim was still in awe of the collection of masterpieces.

"Mark could open his own gallery with these," Tim said to Jeffrey.

"I think he has plans to do just that," Jeffrey said. "Keep the wolf away from the door, so to speak."

Mark had now joined them, his trademark glass of whisky in his hand.

"Absolutely right, Jeffrey. In fact, I'll be looking for a curator in case you know of anyone."

Tim remained silent but inwardly was thinking that looking after such a wonderful collection would be his dream job.

"I say, Tim." Mark looked directly at him. "Didn't Jeffrey say you were an artist?"

"I studied at art school, but never achieved anything on this level."

Mark laughed. "I'm not asking you to paint, old chap, just look after them, love them, keep a record, you know the sort of thing. And if I do decide to open the gallery to the public, you'd be in charge. What about it?"

Tim was rather taken aback. "Well, I'd... I mean, I would adore to but—"

Jeffrey stopped him mid-sentence. "Darling, don't forget we live in Chelsea. It would be a hell of a commute down here."

"But you could both live here. There's a cottage on the estate. Jeffrey, you could completely redesign the interior in your impeccably good taste..."

Tim realised that, of course, Jeffrey was quite right and perhaps a little jealous of Mark making such a proposal to him.

"It's a wonderful idea and very generous of you, Mark, but Jeffrey is quite right. We both need to be in London for our work sadly."

Jeffrey looked at Tim's expression. He knew Tim was disappointed and that he, Jeffrey, was also terrified of losing him. Jeffrey could see no solution, even had he wanted to move to the country, his work was London-based. His clients all had homes in London, although many also had weekend homes in the country. Besides. As a child he remembered his nanny reading *The Town and Country Mouse* to him at bedtime. He never tired of listening to how the town mouse preferred the town and the country mouse preferred the country.

He was definitely a town mouse, enjoying the best restaurants, the theatre, the opera, the architecture, the invitation to gallery openings, the Chelsea Flower Show, the cricket at Lords and all the other delights which this great city had to offer.

Their conversation was brought to a halt by the appearance of a notorious tycoon who strode into the gallery with the confidence of a mediaeval monarch, expecting everyone in the room to focus their attention upon him. His impeccable cream suit made him stand out from the crowd.

"Laurence!" Mark greeted his guest with a hug and a brush of his lips across his cheek. "I thought you were on your yacht, somewhere in the Pacific."

"I was, but unfortunately there was an emergency with one of my companies and I had to fly back for the weekend. Then I remembered your soiree and decided to come along for a bit of relaxation."

"So good to see you," Mark said warmly. "Are you alone?"

"I left the wife and mistress on the yacht." Laurence laughed, refusing a glass of champagne as Jamie passed by with his tray, but bent over and whispered in Mark's ear. "Don't suppose you have any charlie, do you? I feel like blowing my mind."

Mark excused himself and led Laurence out of the room. Jeffrey had overheard Laurence's question.

"Mark certainly seems to know anyone who is anyone," Tim commented to Jeffrey.

"Yes, indeed." Jeffrey took a refill from Jamie. "And some are pretty unsavoury characters."

Tim glanced around the room.

"That chap over there..." Jeffrey gestured towards a stocky, grey-haired male holding court with Peter, the rock star, and his girlfriend Claudia. "He's a journalist and has his own programme on TV. Full of himself. I was at school with him, would you believe, but he's only interested in people who have fame and fortune these days. Last time I was here, I went up to say hello and over my shoulder he caught sight of some well-known racing driver and made a beeline for him, completely dismissing me."

"Awful fella," Tim said, knowing how sensitive Jeffrey was. "But surely he knew you're a famous interior designer?"

At that point, the gong sounded and guests filed into the Napoleon room to take their seats for dinner.

Tim gazed around the room with awe at the huge oil paintings with the theme of the Napoleonic Wars, which were hung upon the heavily embossed papered walls.

Couples were seated opposite each other, which Tim rather resented as he preferred to sit beside Jeffrey. He realised he would have to engage in polite conversation with a complete stranger.

However, he was pleasantly surprised to find the well-known author Casper Armstrong-Greene coming to sit next to him. Casper immediately introduced himself.

"Delighted to meet you," Tim said, returning Casper's firm handshake. "I have to confess I really enjoy your novels." He hoped he didn't sound sycophantic.

Casper was obviously pleased. "Oh, thank you. Did you prefer the first series or the last?"

Tim realised he had not read the books as a series. To be truthful, he had only read three, but he was sincere when he said he had enjoyed them; they were what one would term literary works.

"Er, I'm not sure which series they belonged to, I'm afraid. I read them as individual works."

"Oh, I see," Casper said somewhat dismissively. "Well, they were written in chronological order, otherwise it rather ruins the plot, so to speak."

"Indeed." Tim nodded. "I shall endeavour to complete the series when I return to London."

"Please don't feel you have to say that merely to be polite." Casper lifted his glass in a flamboyant gesture and drank the remains of the champagne.

"No, not at all. I promise you, I really did enjoy the ones I read."

He could feel he was digging himself deeper into a dark hole and Casper already had an air of boredom about him.

They spoke little during the first course and by the second, Casper excused himself and said he had just seen an old acquaintance who appeared to have an empty chair next to him, so he would join him for the rest of the meal.

Tim turned to a rather glamorous middle-aged woman who was seated on his other side. She was dressed in an exotic fashion, layers of colourful chiffon complemented by strands of ethnic beads. Her hair was a grey bob and she spoke with what Tim's mother would have described as a "plummy voice".

"Don't take any notice of Casper." She leant towards Tim in a conspiratorial fashion. "He used to be such a nice young man, but the drugs completely changed him." She took a sip of the white wine which Jamie had just poured for her. "He's a brilliant author though, despite everything."

Tim immediately liked his dining companion. "Yes, I'm afraid I made rather a fool of myself. I told him how much I admired his books and when he asked which ones, my mind went completely blank!"

"Oh well, you know how sensitive these creative people can be. Do you write?"

Tim smiled. "No, afraid not."

"Oh, please don't apologise. I adore writers and musicians and artists, but they are rarely happy souls." She took another sip of wine. Hannah, the housekeeper's daughter who was acting as a waitress for the evening, placed plates of smoked salmon in front of them.

"I take it you are a friend of my son's?" She elegantly picked up her knife and fork.

The table was now full and all the guests began eating.

"Your son?"

"Mark. He gives these soirees regularly. Unfortunately, he has never appeared to have a particular talent himself, but he adores surrounding himself with talented people."

Tim hadn't even been aware that Mark's mother was alive and certainly hadn't expected to meet her this evening.

"He had the best education, of course. Eton and Sandhurst. And I think he enjoyed his spell in the army, but somehow he never settled afterwards. And what do you do… sorry, I don't know your name."

"Tim. I, er, teach art."

"Oh, really? How interesting. Then you must know all about the wonderful paintings here."

"I'm not sure I know about all of them, but it is a magnificent collection."

She finished the salmon and pushed her plate aside, accepting Tim's offer to refill her glass.

"Yes, most of them have been in the family for generations. I have to confess, every time one of our predecessors got into debt, they would sell a painting, but my late husband stipulated in his will that they should be passed on to the next generation."

Tim was suddenly conscious of Jeffrey looking across the table at him. He seemed to have been placed between two young, rather glamorous and overly made-up young women.

Jeffrey was much better at small talk than Tim himself was, but his expression was one of quiet bemusement as the girls appeared to be chattering away to him.

When the main course of lamb from the estate arrived, Lady Botellier turned to the person seated on her left and began a conversation. Tim realised this was correct protocol at dinner parties, but at the same time, he was rather disappointed not to have had a longer conversation with Mark's mother as he had instantly warmed to her and was fascinated to know more about the family history. Instead, he found himself sitting quietly with the seat left by the novelist still empty and no one with whom he could converse. As soon as the main course was finished, Jeffrey, being rather protective, excused himself from his companions and came to sit next to Tim.

"Heavens, what did I do to deserve that?" Jeffrey sat down, clutching a large glass of red wine.

Tim laughed. "I wasn't sure whether you were enjoying yourself or not. They are very glamorous though."

"Darling, you know that is wasted upon me. They did possess a great sense of humour though. Apparently, they present a popular television programme and seemed quite forlorn

when I said I had never watched it."

At that moment, Lady Botellier turned back towards Tim having decided she had done her duty in politely conducting a conversation with the aged art historian on her left.

"Jeffrey." She smiled warmly. "How lovely to see you. Are you well?"

Jeffrey momentarily left his seat and went to give her a kiss upon the cheek.

"Lovely to see you too, Lettuce dear. I see you have already met my partner Tim."

"Such a charming young man, but I didn't realise he was anything to do with you. He's far too good looking," she teased.

Tim moved along a seat so Jeffrey could sit next to Lady Lettuce. Tim reflected that he had never met anyone called Lettuce before.

After dinner, as more champagne flowed freely, the atmosphere was most convivial. Tim also realised that plentiful drugs added to the heady atmosphere and realised how naive he was about the world of drugs. He was used to trying to recognise the pupils at school who were most likely to be addicted or employed as runners for the various gangs of drug pushers, but he had not realised how prevalent they were in certain sections of society. One could say that it was money of the rich individuals who kept the drug barons in business.

Tim actually found himself having a conversation with Pete, the rock star, about the importance of music and art in a civilised society and who was the most important: the artist or the writer. It was obvious that Pete was most erudite but then Tim, reflecting upon the lyrics of his songs, presumed he would be. Jeffrey, meanwhile, was having a most animated discussion about interior design with Claudia.

"I would love you to come and see the pied-à-terre Pete just gave me for my birthday," Claudia was saying enthusiastically, "And perhaps you might even agree to do the interior design for me. I know what I like but I am hopeless at putting it all together."

Jeffrey noticed she had an accent and assumed with her mane of blonde hair that it was Scandinavian. He liked her. There was no pretence about her and she seemed genuinely interested in his work.

"I'd be delighted to come and have a look," he said, allowing a rather exhausted Jamie to replenish his gin and tonic. "Forgive me for prying, but where are you from?"

"Sweden," she replied. "I met Pete when he and his band were on tour in Stockholm. I was one of the models appearing on stage at the beginning of the concert. Afterwards, we just got on so well together that he invited me to come back to London with him."

"How romantic," Jeffrey said. He supposed she knew all about his previous relationships with many beautiful women, a few of whom had born his children. However, who was Jeffrey to moralise. Such behaviour seemed perfectly acceptable these days.

A well-known photographer, who obviously knew Claudia, interrupted their conversation and Jeffrey decided it was time to move on. He was also beginning to feel rather worse for wear and was relieved they were not driving back to London that night.

He was about to catch Tim's eye and suggest they retire to their room when a politician, whom he had met before at one of Mark's soirees, approached him.

George Webster had shown promise at the beginning of his career, but as a young member of the government, he had been seduced by the trappings of success and fame. At one time, George had even been tipped to be the next PM. Sadly, such promise had been short-lived. George and his ambitious wife, both from working-class backgrounds, had fallen prey to the offer of free luxury holidays on millionaires' yachts and in their opulent villas. He had also forgotten that the reason for his entering politics after Oxford was to improve the lives of the hard-working people with whom he had grown up.

Terri Webster enthusiastically embraced the endless offers of freebies from fashion houses and high-class jewellers and even when on loan, conveniently would forget to return the objects. She also enjoyed mixing with celebrities and looked forward to the day when she and her husband would be able to host glamorous parties at Number Ten. Unfortunately for her, greed had overtaken her husband and he had been exposed for indulging in shady deals and banished to the backbenches; all hope of reaching the top position gone.

In disgust and disappointment, Terri had embarked upon an affair with a famous footballer, but when that ended, heartbroken George took her back and now they hung on to what few friends and acquaintances who had stood by them.

Mark had first met George through a mutual friend who was also a supplier of cocaine to the great and the good, and as Mark realised George and Terri knew far too much about his private life, he had no choice but to make sure they were always invited to his parties. For their part, they were grateful to still be invited to a gathering where they could at least boast to the few friends they had left of how they had met a famous actor or pop star.

"Jeffrey, old mate, we were only talking about you the other day, weren't we, Terri?"

"We were." Terri, who had consumed copious glasses of champagne throughout the evening, swayed towards Jeffrey and slung an arm around his neck and proceeded to kiss him full on the lips.

Jeffrey tried to pull away, but feeling rather unstable himself, almost fell into her arms.

"We've bought this bijou apartment in Cannes, but it's in quite a dilapidated state. Belonged to some old biddy in the film world who died and her nephew just wanted to get rid of it asap," George said. "Anyway, it needs the impeccable taste of someone like you, Jeffrey, to bring it to life. We'd pay for your fare down there, of course, and you could stay there for free, of course."

Tim remained silent, unsure as to what Jeffrey's reaction would be.

"Well, I'm rather busy for the foreseeable future." Jeffrey was leaning against Tim's shoulder.

"Oh, darling Jeffrey, you must say yes." Terri put on her best pout, which was supposed to look sexy.

"Can we talk about it another time?" Jeffrey said. "We were actually just on our way to bed and, to be honest, I'm completely knackered."

"Well, promise me you'll think about it," Terri insisted. "We're going home as we don't live far away, but perhaps you could call in for a drink on your way back tomorrow."

"Are you okay to drive, George?" Jeffrey sounded concerned. "Or do you have a driver?"

"I'll be okay," George replied. "Afraid the driver went with all the other perks when I was booted out of the cabinet."

"Such a pain," Terri added.

Five minutes later, Tim steadied Jeffrey up the grand staircase. He couldn't resist asking about how he came to know George and Terri, as it was obvious to him they were not Jeffrey's type of people at all. Jeffrey explained he had met them through Mark and as soon as they heard Jeffrey had actually designed apartments at Kensington Palace, Terri was adamant he should redesign their London townhouse. But, due to unforeseen circumstances, they were forced to sell it and move to the country, so it never happened.

They walked along the wide corridor at the top of the stairs where more paintings hung upon the embossed, crimson walls, looking for the bedroom which they had been allocated.

"I think it was this one." Tim turned to Jeffrey. "Number fifteen."

He placed his hand upon the brass doorknob and pushed the door open. They were both suddenly aware that the opulently furnished room was already occupied as the naked bodies of Jeffrey's companions at dinner sprang from the bed, followed by the muscular, tattooed figure of a famous footballer. The girls' giggles turned to alarm as they hurriedly retrieved their clothes from the Indian carpeted floor and hastened towards the door where Tim and Jeffrey stood somewhat bemused.

"So sorry." The girls hastened past them, trying to hide their giggles.

The footballer was more casual as he put on his shirt and trousers and glittering jacket and sauntered towards the door. Tim and Jeffrey stood aside for him to pass.

"Sorry, mate." He grinned as he exited the room. "Must have got the wrong room."

"Honestly, what a nerve." Jeffrey seemed to have sobered up. "I know the girls are not staying the night as they told me at dinner they had a lift back to town. I suppose with that footballer." Jeffrey's face has turned a shade of crimson and

Tim was concerned about his blood pressure. "I really don't fancy sleeping in soiled sheets."

"I know what you mean," Tim agreed. "Perhaps there'll be some clean ones in the cupboard."

Tim peered into a huge oak wardrobe, which fortunately was stocked with crisp, white sheets and pillows and immediately set about remaking the bed with clean sheets, much to Jeffrey's relief.

The next morning, those guests who had stayed the night emerged at various times to take breakfast in a large oak panelled room. There was an inviting selection of cereals, egg dishes, kippers and marmalades set out on a long sideboard. Everyone helped themselves and then sat at a long oak table, where bowls of colourful fruit were interspersed with homemade jams, croissants and pastries.

Tim found himself standing at the buffet beside Casper, the author who had deserted his table during dinner. He exchanged a brief "good morning", but as Casper was obviously suffering from over-indulging the previous evening and no doubt snorting several lines of cocaine, he did not, unsurprisingly, appear to remember Tim at all, much to Tim's relief.

As Tim returned to the table, he almost spilt his coffee over a very pretty young actress, whom he recognised

"Gosh, I'm really sorry," he stuttered staring into her vivid blue eyes.

"Oh, please don't apologise." She smiled. "I'm hardly awake myself. Wasn't it a wonderful evening?"

"Yes, indeed." Tim nodded, wishing he'd had the chance to speak to this seemingly carefree creature instead of arrogant Casper.

At that moment, Jeffrey caught his eye, impatient for his coffee, so Tim excused himself and joined him at the dining table.

Just before they were about to leave and Jeffrey had gone outside to find their driver, who had insisted upon staying in a local B & B despite being welcome at the house, Mark took Tim aside and told him he would wait a couple of months for Tim's final decision, meaning he was giving him a chance to persuade Jeffrey that he should take the job as curator of Mark's masterpieces.

"What's he going to pay you with? Cocaine?" Jeffrey said huffily as they drove back to London when Tim attempted to broach the subject. "He's got through his fortune, you know.

Lettuce was telling me. She despairs of him and what will happen to the hall."

"Oh, I don't know, Jeffrey. Let's forget it as it upsets you so much. It was just that when I saw all those marvellous paintings, I simply fell in love."

"With the paintings or their owner?" Jeffrey snapped.

"The paintings, of course." Tim took Jeffrey's hand and squeezed it. "Not as much as I love you though."

Jeffrey sighed heavily. "I don't know what I'd do without you." He was close to tears.

"You won't have to, Jeffrey dearest. I told you I'm here for life, as long as you need me."

Jeffrey held Tim's face close to his and kissed him passionately. "Forever," he said softly, as he released him from his grasp.

Sanders, the driver, turned on the car radio and avoided gazing in the mirror to the back of the car. He knew how to be discreet in such matters.

Sometimes one wonders whether fate really does play a part in our lives. Two months later, when Tim knew Mark would have to find another curator for his gallery, Jeffrey, after a boozy day entertaining clients at Ascot, came home complaining of feeling very weird, as opposed to inebriated, and collapsed into Tim's arms. He never recovered consciousness despite the best attempts made by the Brompton Hospital.

Tim was in total shock. He couldn't accept the fact Jeffrey would no longer be there beside him in bed, taking him to the theatre and wonderful restaurants, sharing the joys of exhibitions and art galleries, choosing clothes together but, most of all, giving him so much love and affection and a feeling of contentment and security, much more than Tim ever dreamt of. Now those dreams were shattered.

He called Mark to tell him the sad news and although Mark was genuinely sad when hearing of Jeffrey's death, he immediately saw a release of duty for Tim and the chance of a new life.

"Well, I'm devastated, I have to say. And can only imagine what you are going through, but it's not too unfeeling of me to ask whether you'll now consider my offer. It might even help the process of mourning."

Tim paused. It did seem rather sudden and yet he wasn't offended by Mark's asking him.

"I'd love to, Mark," he said quietly. "When would you like me to start?"

At the end of term, Tim left his teaching job, rented out the house in Chelsea and moved to a cottage on Mark's estate. Mark gave him an office at the hall and he began collating the vast collection of pictures.

When Tim caught up with Eleanor, purely by chance, on a trip to the Royal Academy in London to see a Picasso exhibition, she told him about her favourite class at the comprehensive where she taught and how she truly believed that introducing them to great works of art could change their lives. He realised that in his capacity as guardian of some of the best paintings in the world, he could offer to help her in her endeavour.

Hence the coach trip was arranged for Year 10 to visit the hall.

CHAPTER EIGHT

Eleanor had no doubt Joel and Leila, her star pupils, would benefit hugely from the trip to Botellier Hall. However, she would dearly love it if those in the group who felt life revolved around drugs, alcohol, knives and joining gangs and who were prepared to "die young" as their future held no hope of a different existence were to benefit from the day. She would be elated if the paintings could give them inspiration, raise their expectations, motivate them to make something of their lives and that corny expression of "pursue their dreams".

She knew one or two of her class were already involved in courses run by Prince Charles' charity, The Prince's Trust, which aimed to give the most disadvantaged young people a chance to make the most of their lives. She had every admiration for the prince's aim, but how did one change the lives of young people like Jamal and Jordan, who had never known normal family life? But she hoped, perhaps as the prince did, that she could play a very small part in encouraging them to explore the world of art as a beginning.

One of Mark's circle of acquaintances, whom Tim had met at a weekend social gathering, was Fergal Geary, an Irish poet. Tim had immediately been drawn to Fergal with his soft, Irish voice and lyrical tones. When Fergal began to speak, one always listened. He spoke in an eloquent manner and it was always as if he were telling a story. Fergal was also extremely kind and passionate about what mattered most to him: namely the search for beauty and truth and the sharing of knowledge with those who were interested.

Since becoming curator of the picture gallery, Tim had made it open to the public on certain days and evenings. He had also introduced special events, such as audiences with artists, writers, actors, historians and poets. Fergal was one of the most popular guests and wooed the audience with dramatic renditions of his poetry.

Tim knew that Fergal would be the ideal person to enthuse the young students whom Eleanor was bringing on a school visit.

Having stopped at a picnic spot in a nearby forest, which was a treat in itself, where the class had eagerly eaten their sandwiches and visited the loos, Eleanor ushered them back onto the coach.

Eleanor had provided the ham, cheese, prawn and egg sandwiches as she was only too aware that asking the class to bring their own would have given some of them added pressure. Her choice of various fillings had proved a great success.

"Are we nearly there, miss?" Jamal asked from the back of the bus where he and his companions had spent most of the journey playing games on their phones, instead of looking out of the windows and enjoying the scenery: landscapes of patchwork fields where country crows and pigeons pecked at the newly planted oats and barley seed and further along, dark deep mysterious forests where King Henry VIII no doubt once hunted deer.

"Do you see those large wrought iron gates ahead?" Eleanor asked.

Now everyone did turn to peer out of the coach windows.

"That is Botellier Hall."

Everyone was in awe.

"Wow, it looks like Buckingham Palace."

"What a pad."

"Wouldn't mind living in a place like that, man."

"The owner, the Earl of Botellier, has generously invited you to be his guests and view his magnificent art collection, which his ancestors have acquired over the centuries. So, please remember to thank him and be polite at all times."

The driver spoke into an intercom at the gates, which proceeded to open and they began the journey along the two-and-a-half-mile drive, which led to the hall.

The girls were excited to see deer in the surrounding parkland; most of them had never seen a deer in the flesh.

"I'd like to take one home with me," Leila said longingly to Joel. She remembered, as a child, being amongst the animals on her grandparents' farm first in Yemen and then high in the hills of Iraq.

"Might be a bit cramped." Joel laughed. "And I think they can have quite a temper!"

"Here we are." Eleanor stood up as the coach drew to a halt at the bottom of some rather grand steps The wide steps led up to a most impressive portico shielding an equally grand entrance into the hall.

Eleanor had texted Tim to say they had arrived and he stood at the top of the steps ready to greet them.

"Eleanor, darling." The pair embraced much to the amusement of the teenagers standing behind her, a few stifling giggles.

"Class, this is a very old friend of mine Tim. We were at art school together many years ago."

"Welcome, everyone." Tim nodded as he was greeted enthusiastically with "Hi, Tim". He ushered them all inside.

The gasps, as they stood in the grand, marble floored, high-ceilinged hall, were audible. None of them had ever experienced such a place, apart from perhaps Leila, who had been familiar with beautiful buildings in her hometown before they had been reduced to rubble.

"I prepared some refreshments in the library as I thought you might be hungry after your long journey. This way," Tim said.

Dutifully, they followed him. Eleanor had never known her class speechless before as they entered the oak panelled room where shelves displayed beautifully bound books in the best Florentine leather. She studied the expressions upon their faces. It was joyous to see their reactions, but she also felt sadness that they had lived fourteen and fifteen years of their lives without being aware that such beauty existed. She was also conscious they might easily feel resentful of the wealth of such people, who were able to acquire such stunning homes and fill them with priceless possessions.

Mrs Moreton helped them to pour lemonade and orange squash from glass jugs, keeping an eager eye to make sure not a drop was spilt upon the priceless Persian carpet.

She was needed at the hall more frequently since Tim had arrived and opened it up to one hundred visitors. The pay was not much more but she enjoyed getting out of the house and meeting new people. It was also preferable to staying at home with her husband who, although she was still very fond of him, had become a "grumpy old man" since retiring from his work as the local school caretaker. The problem was, as she often told him, that he had no hobbies and as her mother had always said, a man needs hobbies apart from meeting his mates for a pint in the local pub.

Mrs Moreton noticed the young girl with dark exotic features looking intensely at the carpet beneath her feet.

"This reminds me of home," Leila confided in Joel. "In Yemen and Iraq, we had similar carpets. One of my uncles used to weave them. I remember as a small child how he used to tell me that every carpet told a different story and I loved hearing about them. Sometimes it was people, sometimes animals."

Joel noticed the sadness in Leila's voice and the usual sparkle in her dark eyes was momentarily lost to another world; one which she wanted to remember and yet tried to forget.

Tim made sure he spoke to each individual, asking what their interests were and whether they had any idea of what they would like to do eventually with their lives, although being sensitive to putting them under any pressure.

Eleanor looked on, grateful to Tim for taking such an interest in the young people. It was so important for them to feel that people cared. She was also relieved that she had remembered to confiscate all weapons before they left London, albeit they had been reluctant to hand them over. She had locked them in a cupboard and said they could reclaim them upon their return. She knew it was no use expecting them to go home without the security of their knives. She knew it was wrong and was quietly working upon weaning them off possessing these evil, destructive objects, but until something was done to wipe out knife crime completely, she knew it was of no use banning the possession of weapons.

"How many books in this library, sir?" Joel asked, looking around at the vastness of the floor-to-ceiling mahogany shelves, everyone crammed from end-to-end with hundreds of books. Joel felt small and insignificant as his eyes explored in awe the vision of various coloured, leather spines, bearing gold inscribed titles and containing thousands and thousands of words, the outpouring of thousands of minds over the centuries. Far more than he or anyone could ever read in a lifetime!

"I believe about six thousand five hundred on the last count." Tim smiled. "And don't ask whether I have read them all, as I have to confess, I haven't opened one… yet."

The others laughed. Reading the printed word in a book was a novel concept for many of them in today's world of iPads and computer screens.

"Can we look at one?"

Eleanor turned in surprise as she recognised Jamal's voice behind her. He was the last person she expected to pose such a question.

"Of course." Tim walked towards the shelves. "Any particular subject? History, English literature, drama, mathematical theory, philosophy, poetry…"

"Yeah, that would be good," Jamal said, nodding.

"Poetry?" Tim checked this was his chosen subject.

A couple of his mates sniggered.

"What about an anthology?" Tim suggested.

A puzzled expression crossed Jamal's face.

"It's a compilation, a mixture, if you like, of different poets. Then you can decide which ones you like and those you don't."

Jamal nodded as Tim mounted the library steps.

Eleanor was showing the others some of the beautiful pieces of antique furniture. She thought it better that Jamal and Tim were left alone, otherwise Jamal might feel self-conscious in front of his classmates.

Tim descended the steps and handed Jamal the heavy, leatherbound, gilt edged volume of poems.

Jamal opened the book, taking care not to crease or damage any of the delicate pages.

"How old's this book, sir?"

"Well, a lot older than you, Jamal, and I suspect me too, even though you might find that hard to believe."

Jamal laughed.

"If you look inside the cover, there should be a page saying where and when it was printed. I suspect it is probably a first edition, so that makes it quite valuable."

Jamal was studying the page containing the publisher's name.

Tim peered over his shoulder. "There's the date at the bottom of the page... 1798 and it is a first edition."

"Wow." Jamal was impressed. "That's well old."

"Even older than me." Tim laughed. "Why don't you look in the index and choose a poem. What do you like? Romance, adventure...?"

"Nah, not romance," Jamal responded. "Is there anything on space demons?"

"Afraid not, Jamal. These poets lived quite a time before space travel, but I'm sure we can find something with an exciting theme." Tim was looking with him. "What about this one? 'The Rime of the Ancient Mariner' by Samuel Taylor Coleridge. It's what we call a ballad. It tells a story."

"What's a mariner, sir?"

"It's another name for a sailor and this is the story of an old sailor whose ship is driven by storms towards the South Pole. He then crosses the Pacific Ocean where the mariner kills a huge seabird which is following, called an albatross, and realises he has done a bad thing…"

"People shouldn't kill things?" Jamal said.

"Exactly," Tim agreed. "And in the ballad, we learn of what happens once the old sailor has killed the bird. Poetry is always better read aloud and I have just the person to do this. In fact, he should be here any moment."

"It isn't Coleridge, is it?" Another young boy had joined them and had been standing nearby listening.

"No, no." Tim laughed gently. "Most of the poets in this volume died a long time ago. In fact, before the date it was published. We do still have modern day poets and my friend Fergal, who is from Ireland, is one of those."

"Does he make a lot of money?" Alfie, the small pale boy with miniature features and a floppy fringe falling across his forehead and getting in the way of his eyes, asked.

"There's not a great deal of money in writing poetry, no," Tim answered his question, "But it is possible to make a living. It's the same with artists. Only a few become rich and famous. Many have to work at other jobs in between painting." He paused. "But it's not really about making money, is it? If you are really happy in what you are doing, that in itself is priceless. Money can't buy you contentment and peace of mind."

"Money can buy you a palace like this though," Alfie persisted, "And all these thousands of books and all the treasures inside it."

"Well, that's true," Tim said, "But having a big house and lots of possessions doesn't necessarily guarantee you'll be happy."

He could see Alfie wasn't convinced. Coming from a high-rise block of flats situated on an estate where he shared a bedroom with his mum and baby brother and was scared of leaving the flat every day for fear of being bullied, he would give anything to have a place to live, just a quarter of the size of Botellier Hall, with its own grounds where he could walk and explore knowing he wasn't in danger.

"Me mum says she don't know for how much longer she can put food in our mouths. We don't know where me dad went and her job in the hospital kitchens don't pay much."

Tim was humbled and felt how insensitive he had been. Who was he to preach to a young lad who had known nothing but poverty in his young life. Alfie's mother probably relied upon food banks to get through. Although Tim himself had come from a working-class background in the Welsh Valleys, they had never wanted for anything and home was a secure and happy place.

Tim was quite relieved to see Fergal enter the room as he would be saved, for the time being, from answering any more questions. Fergal hobbled towards the group, having sprained his ankle whilst tripping over the lead of his dog on the way home from the local pub one night. He had a somewhat dishevelled look, having no interest whatsoever in clothes, although he was partial to wearing the odd colourful waistcoat. He had a collection of these garments bequeathed from his late father, a country lawyer, whose trademark was his waistcoats. His thick, shoulder-length, dark hair was greying at the temples. His blue eyes twinkled in a childlike expression of excitement on the night before Christmas.

"Fergal, just in time. Jamal here wanted to look at a poetry book and we were perusing this eighteenth century anthology when he came across 'The Rime of the Ancient Mariner' and I said perhaps you would read it for him and Alfie." Tim gestured towards Alfie whose eyes darted from Tim to Fergal, taking in every word they spoke.

"Hello, Jamal." Fergal shook the boy's hand and turning to Alfie did the same. "I'd be delighted to read Coleridge's ballad. Shall we go and perch beside the fireplace over there? I think that would be a suitably intimate setting and if anyone else would like to join us, please feel welcome."

At first, only Joel and Leila stepped forwards but as soon as Fergal began reading in his lilting, seductive Irish tones, gradually the rest of the group manoeuvred themselves towards the huge, open fireplace where Fergal was in his element and enjoying the full attention of his young audience.

"Water, water, everywhere, nor any drop to drink," Fergal read. "Slimy things did crawl with legs upon the slimy sea."

At these lines, several of their faces contorted into expressions of fear and disgust.

"This is an unexpected treat, Tim. Thank you." Eleanor stood beside her old friend. "They are taking in every word."

Fergal was in his element, delivering each line with dramatic effect. As he neared the end of the ballad, the tension rose.

"He prayeth best, who loveth best, all things both great and small. For the dear God who loveth us, He made and loveth all."

There was an unexpected round of applause. Eleanor and Tim were delighted.

When he had finished, Fergal asked how many of them had understood the ballad and what it was about. Many hands went up eager to offer opinions.

"How did you find it?" Fergal asked. "Did it make you feel happy or sad or both?"

"Sad!" Alfie said.

"But it turned out all right in the end," Jamal added.

Leila held her hand up. "Excuse me, but do you know 'Kubla Khan'?"

"Yes, young lady, indeed I do." Fergal smiled at the pretty young girl with exotic looks and began to quote, "'In Xanadu did Kubla Khan a stately pleasure-dome decree...' Are you acquainted with the work?"

"I learnt it at school in Yemen," Leila replied.

"And did you enjoy it?"

"Yes, very much."

"Well, young lady, perhaps we can read it together some time," Fergal offered.

"I would like that."

"Right, well, I am sorry to hurry you on," Eleanor announced, "But after that splendid rendition, I think we should be making our way to the picture gallery."

The students seemed much more relaxed than when they had arrived and had been in awe of their grand surroundings. They followed Tim along a corridor leading to a palatial marble staircase, at the top of which they found themselves in a long gallery. The walls displayed gilt framed oil paintings and watercolours and when they looked up at the ceiling that too was decorated with cherubic figures and depictions of revered poets wearing laurels around their heads, famous Greek philosophers and Roman historians.

Jamal stood transfixed and took a deep breath. "Are these the real paintings the artists done?" he asked Tim.

Alfie, standing beside him, eagerly awaited Tim's reply.

"Oh, indeed, yes," Tim said. "Every one is an original."

Again, there was almost complete silence as the whole class gazed in admiration at the pictures.

Tim knew there were far too many paintings for them to explore in one visit, so he had decided to concentrate upon three and explain the subject of each and how the artist had executed them.

He led them towards the first canvas. In richly coloured oils, it showed a medieval princess, complete with crown, dressed in a plum-coloured velvet and fur trimmed cloak with a dress of satin and silk. There was a turreted, grey stoned castle in the distant background and a hedge of brightly coloured roses in the foreground.

"This is from what we call the Flemish School," Tim began. "It was painted in the fifteenth century in Flanders. Does anyone know where Flanders is?"

"Please, sir." A young girl with freckles and red golden hair hanging almost to her waist put her hand up. The others turned round. They were not used to Amy, a quiet, shy girl, ever speaking in class. "It's in Belgium."

"Quite right." Tim smiled. "And you are?"

"Amy." She bowed her head almost embarrassed.

Tim observed that Amy could almost identify with the figure in the painting: the same colouring, the same delicate features. Perhaps that was what had inspired her to speak.

"Is there anything in particular you notice about the young girl in this picture?"

Several answered at once.

"Posh clothes," Alfie called out.

"Living in a big castle," Jamal added.

"Delicate features." It was Leila who spoke.

"Yes, well done," Tim said. "You have all observed different aspects and Leila mentioned delicate features. This was very much the fashion of paintings at the time. Notice the tiny rosebud mouth, the small eyes and refined nose. The artist has paid great attention to detail. It was an idealistic period for artists and they would experiment with perspective. Hence you see the castle right in the background, but not in true perspective." Tim allowed a moment for them to absorb the detail of the painting. "The artist was a man called Jan van Eyck."

"Was he famous?" Joel asked.

"Yes, he was well-known and, of course, today his paintings sell for a lot of money."

"How much?" It was Alfie who spoke.

"Well," Tim said, "They are usually sold in an auction and that depends upon how many people bid for them, but some paintings can go for millions of pounds..."

"Wow..." There was a low whisper within the group.

"However, we shouldn't really be judging the paintings by what they are worth. It's how clever the artists are, the techniques they use and, of course, the pleasure they give to those who gaze upon them."

Tim did not add that he knew plenty of people who bought paintings purely for investment without having any understanding of the work at all.

There were more questions, which pleased Tim and delighted Eleanor, who looked on like a mother hen with pride in her chicks.

"Take your time," Tim said, "And when you are ready, we'll move on to our next picture."

"She's very beautiful," Leila remarked as she looked at the painting.

"Not as beautiful as you." Joel surprised himself with his sudden comment.

Leila smiled, secretly pleased, but also a little embarrassed. "Oh, thank you, but I think she is much better looking."

At that point, the class began to move on, much to Leila's relief, as she noticed one of the bigger boys smirking, who must have heard Joel's remark.

Tim ushered them in front of a medium sized, gilded framed picture.

"This is the Renaissance period," Tim explained. "Artists had discovered a great deal more about technique, colour, light and space."

The subject was a young girl playing a lute with the pages of music laid on a table before her beside a bowl of brightly coloured fruit, which looked good enough to eat. It was the same painting which Peter Darcy had admired at Mark's party and Tim remembered how Peter had told Claudia, his girlfriend, about the painter.

"Who painted it?" Joel asked.

"Well, a man named Caravaggio painted the original, which is in a famous gallery in Italy. This was probably painted by students who helped him, but nevertheless it is very good."

"Who was Cara..." Jamal stumbled over the name. "Caravaggio?"

"Well," Tim began, "Caravaggio came from a very poor family in Milan. His mother brought all five of her children up on her own."

"Sounds like my mum." It was Marek, a usually quite young boy, who spoke. Eleanor looked on sympathetically.

"Then you know, young man, that it is not easy to pay for food and clothes for so many children." His voice was gentle. "His mother died when he was about to start his apprenticeship. He wasn't a very happy young man. He had a bad temper and was always getting into fights. In fact he was accused of murdering a man and had to run away from Rome, where he had been earning a living painting frescoes in the churches and religious paintings for the clergy."

"Phew," Jamal said, "Did he get put in prison?"

"He did eventually." Tim nodded. "He ended up in a small seaside town where he was caught and put in jail. But when they let him out, he caught malaria as there were a lot of mosquitoes in the little port and he died. He was thirty-eight years old. Although many people thought he had been poisoned."

"That's the same age as my mum," Alfie said.

"Well, luckily we don't have malaria here," Tim reassured him. "But he painted a lot of wonderful pictures in his short life."

"The fruit looks real," Alfie said.

"Indeed it does. Well spotted, Alfie."

Alfie blushed although he was delighted Tim had praised him. He could not remember anyone complimenting him upon anything.

"It looks good enough to eat," Alfie added.

"I like the music," Joel said. "It's very clever the way he has painted the notes."

"Exactly," Tim said. "And what about the figure playing the flute?"

"She's cool, man," a tall boy from the back of the group commented.

"Well," Tim said, "Would you be surprised if I said it wasn't a girl, but a boy?"

Alfie covered his mouth with his hand and stifled a giggle, nudging Jamal who stood beside him.

Tim now had everyone's attention. "Artists would often get young boys to pose for them but dress them in female clothes. It's rather like in the theatre. Females were forbidden to be actresses and so all the female parts were played by boys."

"Even in Shakespeare?" Jamal enquired.

"Especially in Shakespeare," Tim replied. "Think of *Romeo and Juliet*."

"Urgh, that's gross." Jordan's face contorted into a look of disgust.

This caused great amusement and everyone pushed forward in order to get a closer look at the canvas and its subject.

"Right, when you have finished looking at this picture, we'll go on to the third one I have chosen. I am sorry we don't have time to look at more, but you'll have to come back and visit us again."

"Yeah!" Alfie said enthusiastically.

The final painting which Tim had chosen was from an English painter in the nineteenth century, although the artist was unknown. It was a scene from the Industrial Revolution and set in a boiling hot furnace where women and small children were expected to turn hot coals.

"So," Tim began, "This painting's subject is very different, I think you'll agree. Anyone like to guess where it might be or when it was painted?"

Everyone focused upon the painting, apart from a couple of the girls at the back who were still giggling at a huge painting of a naked Hercules which was hung nearby.

"Is it when children were made to work in the mines and factories?" Joel said, hoping to impress Leila.

"Quite right," Tim said. "It was a period known as the Industrial Revolution which took place in England in the late 1770s until the 1800s. It changed a great deal. Much of the work men did on the land was now done with machines and people went to work in factories, cotton mills and coal mines. This watercolour of women and children working in an iron furnace is from that time."

"What about school?" Alfie asked.

"School wasn't compulsory and many parents needed their children to earn money, so they would work instead. Some of them as young as three years old."

"Wow." Alfie was speechless and Tim had the attention of the class.

"I'm sure you have learnt about this in your history lessons. What do you think it must have been like working in that furnace in the painting?"

"Hot," Jamal said.

"Dirty," another boy shouted.

"Very hot and dangerous."

"Did they really take babies with them?" Leila asked, horrified, as the burning red flames reminded her of the bomb explosions and fires at home.

"Yes," Tim explained, "Because the men would be working down the mines to get the coal and the women and children worked in the furnace and had no one to leave their babies with."

"It seems very cruel," another young girl added.

"It was and working-class people led very hard lives," Tim said. "We may think we suffer now sometimes in our lives, but I don't think the hardship is as bad as it was then."

Eleanor stepped forwards. "Well, everyone, I'm afraid our coach is waiting for us, so I think we should start to make our way outside."

"Oh," they chorused in disappointment.

"You can come again." Tim smiled at Eleanor who thanked him. She had hoped it would inspire and motivate the art class but she had never expected such a positive outcome.

On the return journey to London, the students chatted enthusiastically about what they had seen. Eleanor texted Tim to thank him and tell him what an impression he had made.

CHAPTER NINE

Arriving back at school, Eleanor told them to wait whilst she went to the cupboard and, taking the objects she had confiscated in the morning, returned them to the owners. Joel hesitated before accepting his knife.

"You don't have to take this," Eleanor said quietly. She had made sure they were alone before handing it to him. "It won't go anywhere. I could leave it in the cupboard."

He paused before replying. "Yeah, if you don't mind, miss. I'll leave it for now."

Eleanor was relieved as she replaced the kitchen knife.

"Goodnight then." She turned, smiling, to face Joel.

"Thank you for today. It was wicked," Joel said.

As he turned to leave, he saw Leila waiting in the corridor for him.

They walked silently across the common until it was the spot where they went separate ways.

"It was brilliant today, wasn't it?" Leila said.

"Yes, it was," Joel agreed.

They were both tired yet elated by their shared experience.

"See you tomorrow then," Joel said.

"Yes." She smiled. "Perhaps you would like to come and eat with us some time?" she added shyly.

"Yes, I'd like that."

He put his rucksack on his back and started walking in the direction of his home. He couldn't wait to tell his mother and Tony about the visit to the grand hall and all the stunning paintings. He knew Tony would be interested as he had been to art school before he joined the band and had collected original paintings, partly as an investment but also because he appreciated them.

Joel thought that perhaps he would like to become an artist, although he realised it wasn't an easy career choice, but he did have a passion for painting and there were jobs where he could use it, such as book illustration for example. His head was buzzing with all these ideas as he strode across the common where a milky moon had crept into the greying sky above.

He turned the corner to make his way along the high street, inhaling the various aromas of restaurants and takeaways offering Chinese, Indian, Greek and other varieties of food.

He realised he was feeling quite hungry and was tempted to stop and pick up a Big Mac but his mum may have something prepared.

Suddenly, he heard voices raised in anger followed by piercing screams, shattering the tranquillity of the early evening air.

Then, as he approached the tube station entrance, he saw a group of older boys, some of whom he recognised from school, including Jordan, who towered above the others. They appeared to be attacking a figure whom they had surrounded in a circle, like some frightened animal about to be set upon by a pack of wolves.

He wondered whether he should turn back and avoid the commotion, but at that moment, he caught sight of the petrified figure, lying in a foetal position on the ground, pleading for mercy.

Instinctively, Joel ran towards the gang.

"Keep out, Joel." It was Jordan who gave the command. "This ain't nothing to do with you."

"He's my mate," Joel persisted. "He's not done anything wrong, let him go."

"I said, keep your f—king nose out of it," Jordan retorted loudly. "It don't concern you. We have business with this little shit. He's disobeying orders. No one defies me. All that arty farty art given him grand ideas, innit." Jordan looked down at Jamal and spat, aiming for his face.

Joel could not understand how Jordan could behave in such a cruel manner, especially after the enjoyable day they had all experienced. Even Jordan had seemed impressed by some of the paintings and appeared genuinely interested in Tim's commentary about the artists and their subjects.

"I'll go instead of him," Joel said, realising Jamal must be one of Jordan's runners too. His heart began to beat faster. He wanted to get away, but he couldn't leave Jamal to be beaten up by these thugs.

"He's not going anywhere!" Jordan lurched at Jamal with his foot, kicking him in the small of his back as he lay, curled in a foetal position, pleading for mercy.

Jamal's dark eyes looked up imploringly as he recognised Joel looking down upon him.

Joel remembered he had refused to take his knife back from Miss Wells when they had returned to school. He had felt good about himself as he had walked with Leila. He was always anxious she would find out he usually carried a knife. Now he regretted not having it with him.

Jordan had already thrust his knife into Jamal's shoulder and the blood was pouring from the wound covering his clothes and the ground beneath him. Joel could see the almost evil expression upon Jordan's face as if determined to kill his victim.

Joel lurched at Jordan in a vain attempt to take his knife from him.

"He's defenceless. He can't fight back, leave him," he shouted, surprising himself at the force of his voice.

"Yeah? And what you gonna do about it?" Jordan snarled.

His mates guffawed. They were like baying animals, Joel thought.

"Joel, help me," Jamal wailed. He was clutching his bleeding shoulder, but at any attempt he made to stand up, he was forcefully pushed back down.

Joel made another desperate attempt to relieve Jordan of his weapon. For a moment, he had distracted Jordan and managed to pull Jamal to his feet.

"Run," Joel shouted to Jamal, pushing him forwards.

Just as Jamal made his escape, he heard an excruciating cry of pain and, turning back, saw Jordan had knifed Joel in the chest. He panicked, looking around searching for any visible sign of help. There were quite a few people strolling up and down the street and even a few bedraggled commuters surfacing from the underground, one of which was a middle-aged man dressed in a suit, shirt and tie, carrying an expensive-looking leather case.

"Mister, my mate's been stabbed. He needs an ambulance." In a panic, he grabbed the man by the arm only to be pushed away as if he was being attacked by some vermin. "Please," Jamal implored, close to tears. "They took my mobile. I need to get help."

Reluctantly, the stranger took out his phone. "I'll call an ambulance, but that's all I'm prepared to do. You young thugs bring it upon yourselves."

"Please, just call an ambulance. I think he's dying!"

The man was already speaking into his phone, giving his location.

"There. Satisfied? I'm not getting involved any further. It's on its way." He turned and strode off in the opposite direction.

Jamal felt helpless.

Turning back, he noticed Jordan and his gang had made their escape, leaving Joel unconscious on the pavement in a deep pool of dark red blood.

Two women walked past on their way to the pub on the corner. They stopped briefly and looked around to see if anyone was doing anything about the young boy bleeding lying in the street.

Jamal ran over, clutching his own shoulder which was still very painful. "I've called an ambulance," he said, looking down at Joel.

"Oh, well, as long as someone's coming," one woman said, hovering on her high heels. Noticing Jamal's wounded shoulder, she added, "We'll be off then." She marched away arm-in-arm with her friend.

Jamal heard the sound of an ambulance as it appeared around the corner and sped to a halt. The medics jumped out immediately and checked Joel was still breathing. From the expression on their faces, Jamal could see it was serious. Gently, they lifted him onto a stretcher and into the ambulance.

"You come too, matey. You've got a nasty wound there which needs treating."

"He was trying to protect me," Jamal explained on the point of breaking down.

The men helped him into the ambulance and sat him next to the stretcher upon which Joel's limp and battered body lay. The paramedics started to perform life-saving procedures upon their patient.

The older man seemed be staring down at Joel in a strange manner; his face almost contorted in pain.

"This your mate?" He turned to Jamal.

Jamal nodded. "He just saved my life. He'll be all right, won't he?" He was trying to hold back the tears.

The strong arms were working on the young, damaged body, desperate to bring it back to life.

"Is his name Joel?" The deep voice was full of emotion.

"Yes, it is, sir. Do you know him?"

The emotional torture was obvious upon the man's face.

"He's my son." His dark once handsome face looked gravely at his colleague, who confirmed there was no longer a pulse or a heartbeat. "My lost son." His voice choked as the tears rolled down his cheeks and he fell to his knees beside Joel's lifeless body.

The local church was full to capacity for Joel's funeral. His death had been reported on local television and film crews were covering the event. Token politicians had appeared on news programmes, repeating the same platitudes as they always did when a young life was tragically lost to knife crime. There was always plenty of talk but little action.

Eleanor Wells, Joel's beloved art teacher, spoke of the loss of a budding talent who would have made a great contribution to society.

A tearful Leila spoke of the loss of her best friend and soulmate, so full of compassion. She then bravely sang a Yazidi folk song from her childhood, which brought the congregation to tears. The song was to have been included on the album which Tony was recording with Leila as a surprise for her mother.

The vicar spoke about the evils of drugs and knife crime, which was in danger of destroying all that humanity stood for. Reverend Tom Morgan had instantly recognised Eleanor Wells as she stood in the pulpit; older, it was true, but still with brilliant blue eyes and an enigmatic smile, reminiscent of the Mona Lisa painting.

Eleanor, overcome with grief and emotion, had barely cast a glance in Tom's direction. It was not until several days later, when looking through the order of service, that she noticed the name of the vicar and, for a moment, wondered whether the young man who once aspired to tread the boards had decided to dedicate his life to the Church instead. She smiled to herself and supposed, if it was the case, preaching to the masses was a form of acting anyway. Although she suspected his congregation consisted of no more than a handful of those souls praying for salvation.

Gemma sobbed throughout the service, unable to speak and leaning heavily upon Tony's shoulder.

Finally, Joel's father took his place in the pulpit and fought back tears as he spoke of the birth of his beautiful son being the best experience of his life, of the love and tenderness he instantly felt for this new born, innocent, human being and the plans which flew around his head like feathers floating along a spring breeze. He would teach him to play football, ride a bike, swim, play the guitar and later share a pint in the pub with his grown-up son.

Sadly, that wasn't to be and through his own foolishness his dreams, and those of his young son, had been shattered.

"Remember..." The deep rich tones of his voice, breaking with emotion, echoed around the Saxon walls of the church. "Make sure you are word perfect before you walk onto the stage of life!"

*"They do not easily rise out of obscurity
whose talents straitened circumstances obstruct at home."*
Juvenal, Roman poet (c. 55–127 AD)

*"If we are to reach real peace in this world,
we shall have to begin with the children."*
Mahatma Gandhi (1869–1948)

Printed in Great Britain
by Amazon